Marlee Jane Ward is a writer, reader and weirdo living in Melbourne. She grew up on the Central Coast of New South Wales and studied Creative Writing at the University of Wollongong. In 2014 she attended the Clarion West Writers Workshop in Seattle, Washington. She likes dreaming of the future, cats, and making an utter spectacle of herself.

You can find her short stories in the Ticonderoga Press *Hear Me Roar* Anthology, *Interfictions* and *Mad Scientist Journal*.

Twitter: @marleejaneward
Facebook: www.facebook.com/marleejaneward
Website: marleejaneward.com

Welcome to
ORPHANCORP

MARLEE JANE WARD

enjoy!

♡

Mel Jue Ward

First published in Seizure by Xoum in 2015
Xoum Publishing
PO Box Q324, QVB Post Office,
NSW 1230, Australia

www.seizureonline.com
www.xoum.com.au

ISBN 978-1-921134-58-6 (print)
ISBN 978-1-921134-59-3 (digital)

Cataloguing-in-publication data is available from the
National Library of Australia

Internal design and typesetting © Xoum Publishing 2015
Cover design by David Henley

Edited by Zoya Patel

*Viva La Novella 3 was made possible through the generous support of
Pamela Hewitt and Xoum Publishing*

To anyone who has ever felt like they were too much.
You aren't, you are just enough.

I twist my hand at a weird angle to get to the itch on my wrist below the shackle. I mean, they call them 'the Consequences of movement violations', but shackles is what they are. When I forget to refer to them as such I get 'the Consequences of speech violations', which is pretty much just a gag. No one cares what I call that because everything sounds the same with a mouthful of rubber, doesn't it?

The bus is ancient and jammed with kids, skinny bums squeezed onto the bench seats. The bus is far noisier than the kids, the whole thing filled with a riot of squeaks and rattles and the odd bang from somewhere inside the engine, while us kids keep our mouths shut and our eyes wide, staring straight ahead. Sweat makes a thin layer between my thighs and the cracked vinyl and my bum aches, pressed into the unpadded bench seat. I bounce hard on my arse bones with every pothole jolt.

No one makes eye contact with me. I'm not the only one shackled . . . sorry, *facing Consequences*, but I am the only one gagged. Sometimes my mouth just starts going and even though in my head I'm all like, *shut up, oh just shut up,* I can't help myself.

We slow and the bus drags itself up to the curb, backfires and dies with a rumble-thud. Everyone kinda cranes their eyes slightly to the left. The Uncle up front glares, on a hawk-eye lookout for any minor infraction of the head-turning variety. They put the thickest, stupidest ones on transport duties, usually as a punishment. They like to make us pay for that. I've been enjoying this one's company for fifteen hours of this broiling hell-trip back to Sydney and when he motions for us to stand and file off, I make sure to catch his arm with one of the strings of drool that have spilled out the sides of my gagged mouth.

'It's been a pleasure,' I say, but it comes out all garbled.

'No talking,' he barks, looking like he wishes he could gag me a second time.

We line up on the footpath beside the bus. The sun is going down and everyone's always tired and grumpy as hell after a transfer, but they've got to stick to procedure, don't they? We all wind out our wrists and ankles as they scan our armband codes and make sure no one's pissed off or died during the trip. It happens.

I take a moment to look over the facility, though

I'm not sure why I bother. Every Verity House is the same — a big grey box straddling an entire city block. It's like they knock them together off-site and heli them in or something. Maybe they do, I don't know. Broome or Blacktown, Albury, Cairns or that one they say is on that island down in Tassie, it doesn't matter. The dining hall is always to the right of the dorms; the watch quarters have those thick, double-brick walls that mean they're easy to sneak past if the door's closed; the bathrooms are sweet little Kidcam blind spots where I can read a non-reg book on my tab, have a cry or a quick-and-dirty interlude up against the wall without facing any of the related Consequences. In their hurry to manufacture heartless functionality, they've made me a home.

I breathe in, scanning the familiar rise and fall of the walls. I take every tiny victory I can, because eventually they add up.

Small victories are all you get in an Orphancorp.

SEVEN DAYS

'Miri . . . Mirya . . . Miriiyanan Mahoney?'

I hold up my shackled hands and wave them a bit. The Auntie, a red-headed woman wider than she is tall, comes over to remove the Consequences piece by piece. I wriggle my wrists and hinge my mouth open and closed to work out the ache in my jaw.

'That's a mouthful of a name, isn't it?'

'It means star. Shooting star,' I tell her, like she'll care, and I wipe the twin spills of spit off my chin with the hem of my shirt.

'So, you're some kinda big shot, are ya? A shooting bloody star?' the Auntie asks, shaking her head and paging through her tab.

'Nah. People just call me Mirii.'

'So, Mirii, what didja say to get the gag? You got a dirty mouth or what?'

I do. In my head I swear *a lot* but the Consequence of profanity is a write up. We work around it. Everything fun is a fugging infraction around here.

I don't want to tell her what I said because she'll probably slam a mark against my name and I *just* got here but I don't have much choice because the big oaf who gagged me in the first place is walking past and he puts a boot into the back of my knee that drops me to the ground.

'Likes to run her mouth, this one,' he says.

'I just pointed out the sweat-marks on Uncle Barry's arse to the bus while he was installing my hands into those Consequences there,' I say, crawling up to my knees and gesturing to the shackles in her hands. 'I mean, I shouldn't have mentioned it; it's pretty noticeable on its own. He's got a big bum.'

They both look down at me and he sinks the boot in once more for good measure before he wobbles off, red faced and sweaty-arsed.

'You're due for Age Release in a week, yeah? You might need to get a hold of your mouth before then.'

'Yeah.' She's got a point, but shiz, if I could control my mouth even the littlest bit, I reckon I mighta done it already.

'So, why'd they bother with the transfer?' she asks.

'I don't know. Why do you guys do anything?'

The Auntie laughs at that. 'You've got a pretty colourful file, little star. We're desperate for Nannies, but the notes say you can't be trusted with kids. You don't like kids?'

'Nope.'

'Nah, me neither. You should come work for us when you age out.' She cackles at that, like she made a super clever joke or something but it's not even funny, right? It's true. Aunties and Uncles must hate kids.

Kids. Shiz. Way to make my blood run cold. They cry and cough and tug my pants, seeking comfort I've got no idea how to give them. It's not their fault, those poor dumb jerks. I did the same when I was their age.

The Auntie scrolls further. 'We're gunna put you into electrical manufacture. You seem to bugger that up less than anything else. Think of it as a parting gift from Verity House.'

'Yeah, thanks,' I say, acting evasive and stuff, but I'm way glad. Tinkering with machines is my thing. Circuit boards and wiring comfort me: they make sense when nothing else does.

'Report at 8 a.m. to the E-wing for work detail. You do school?'

'Yep.'

'Figured. You've got a smart mouth. Classes start at six. Be on time or they won't let you in.'

She moves on to the shy cluster of toddlers next in line. The snotnose little bastards are all sobbing and piddling themselves because half of them have probably just been rounded up off the streets. Even if they were born into an Orphancorp, they're still too little to know what's going on. They let them cry. They let them cry up until they're about six, then after that, crying's an infraction.

The Auntie huffs and puffs until she's crouched down over her huge gut, giant bosom all mashing up into her chin, and she holds up the tab so that the little tykes can see. They stare, saucer-eyed, and a colourful cartoon starts playing.

'Hey kids! Welcome to Verity House!'

—

We shuffle up the steps and through the big red doors. The hallway's the usual concrete slapped over with pastel paint, gone all grimy. What's with that weird pinky-peach chalky colour? Everything's slicked with it – they've gotta buy it by the tonne. Right by the door are the offices for administration and there are heaps of Aunties and Uncles lazing around, joking and laughing, getting fatter by the second, probably thinking up a bunch of nasty schemes to torture us with later. The floor is cream linoleum, scuffed and grey up the edges and I drag my feet over it, leaving little rubber marks. Off to the right is the dining hall and it's already buzzing with the dinner shift of hungry kids who glance up at us and then look away, back into their plates of whatever crap it is they're serving us tonight.

The nursery is the first door on the left and it's

jammed full of crying blobs from ages brand new to just big enough to know better. An Auntie leads our squadron of toddlers off into the room and through the door I see one of the Nannies shake a curly-headed blond wobbler off from clutching at her leg.

'Go away! Just bugger off!' she screams down to him.

The little dude falls splat on his big nappied bum and starts to wail and the Nanny looks up at me as I pass, her eyes scooped out deep with desperation. She's knocked up herself, pretty far along too, dressed in one of those hideous pink preggo-tunics they make the expectants wear and in no time at all she'll be adding her own spawn to the throng.

Fugg me, what a sad little tableau.

I worked extra duties for ten months to get the implant in my arm and it was worth the grind and then some. I can't imagine adding a kid to this mess. I'd never forgive myself.

There's two more dorms, for the four-to-sevens and the nine-to-twelves and they keep divvying up my little transport group until there's just me and two other kids shuffling to the teen barracks, clutching canvas backpacks to our chests, our extra pairs of boots dangling from the laces looped through the straps.

I get a relatively unstained mattress on an empty bunk below the big barred window in the Sixteen/

Seventeen district of the teen dorm and I unload my stuff: one mint-green shirt, one pink. Two pants: lavender, and a kind of peach that matches the walls. One sky blue jacket. They dress us in pastels because they think it makes us calmer or something. I really don't know where they're getting this info from 'cause it doesn't seem to do much but make us look fugging stupid and stain up quick as anything. I've also got seven pairs of grey underpants and seven pairs of grey socks because we only get laundry privileges once a week, if we keep out of trouble. All this goes in the empty plastic crate under the bed, this one is blue and says AntipoDairy, Inc on the side. My second pair of boots go to the foot of the bed.

I feel along the edges of my mattress to find the hidey-hole — nothing is sacred to any of these little bastards except the mattress-safe. I jam the only thing I care about inside: a very battered, technologically obsolete and much-modified tablet: my prized possession. I've been working on that biatch for years and I have it just the way I like it. It holds everything I love: my books, saved copies of all my best assignments from the Free School, pictures of arbitrary things in places that I cared a bit about and lost and that I sometimes like to torture myself with. Look, I'm pretty well aware that it's probs a bit sick to love an inanimate object, but honestly, I'm just glad I can love anything at all. My tab, man. It's like a portal to the rest of the world, a window where I can get a glimpse of what could be if I can just make it out of here.

'Hey big star! Dining Hall, now, unless you want to go to bed hungry.' It's the Auntie from before, waddling past the door.

I follow her back down the hall and get in line for my food. The kid at Position One on the Foodservice line looks up at me with one eye. The other looks way over to the left, but lopsided or not, his eyes look kind.

'Just transferred?' he asks and I nod.

He slaps a little extra of the brownish glop on my tray. 'Welcome to Orphancorp.'

I grin. 'Thanks bru.'

'Newbz,' he says, nudging the next kid in the service row and she picks me out a nice roll that isn't too stale or too mouldy and she passes it on with a whisper to the next one who finds me a decent-looking apple. I nod them all thanks and sit down at a half-empty table, digging into what turns out to be a not-too-awful roo stew.

Everyone's all chattery but all of a sudden things go quiet. I look to the door 'cause a hush like this means something pretty dramatic is afoot. But nothing seems to be up, nothing's different except this one girl has come in through the door. She's got real white skin, almost-white hair and she's small, wiry and kinda beat up. She looks around with a sour expression and no one says anything.

'That's Ferguson. Freya Ferguson,' says a kid at my table, even though I didn't ask. She's a ratty little thing in a pale pink beanie, and she jabs her fork towards the bruised-up chick, who's now scowling at the kids on food service as they make her up a plate. 'She escaped a few weeks ago, she's only just got back from Time Out.'

'Oh. Do you guys do comis?'

Time Out is rough and when someone gets back everyone goes up to them and gives their, like, com-miserations, usually just a nod or a fist bump or if you're okay friends maybe a clap on the shoulder or a chest bump. Depends on the kid.

'Yeah, we do. But I don't got no comis for Freya. I hope they beat her up real good.' Ratty curls a lip at her and goes back to chewing the tough lump of roo she's got between her teeth.

I look up at Freya, sat by herself at a table in the corner. Now and then a kid will walk past and give her a nod, but no line of supporters like usual when someone comes back all bruisy and morose from a long stint in Time Out. When I've gnawed my way through the entire bowl of chewy stew, I take my apple and walk past Freya. I give her a nod and put the apple on her table, 'cause I know all too well the dual emotional smackdown of a long pull in TO coupled with being an unpopular fugg, and jeez, everyone could use a present sometimes. She looks up at me and her eyes are the lightest green, like seriously sparkling emerald as shiz and she smiles, revealing a missing canine tooth.

—

The rules for bedtime go like this: everyone needs to be in bed for count, we call it 'tucking in'. An Auntie or Uncle ticks our names off a checklist on their tab. The Auntie on watch tonight is the big ginger chick from earlier. Her name's Auntie Beverly but all the kids call her Aunt Bev and she pretends she hates it but you can tell she fugging loves it because she flushes an even redder red whenever we say it.

Once lights are out and the door's locked, we can do whatever we like as long as we don't leave. I mean, we can, someone's always got a shifty set of keys that they scrape up in the metalshed, but that's just for special occasions, birthdays and stuff, though in a place like this it's always someone's birthday.

'Where you transfer from?' asks a rake of a girl with a mop of curly black hair and bloodshot black eyes. The 'one size' PJ's they give us swamp her and she's tied knots in the shoulders of the threadbare cotton to keep it from falling right off.

'Orange,' I say and bring my pillow to the cluster they've all huddled theirs into.

'Oh, I been out at Orange,' says a bru about my age

with sunbleached hair, tanned skin, a sixer and guns that he flaunts, shirtless. A gardener for sure, and hot. He's got a righteous grin with a chipped front tooth.

'Was Uncle Jerry there when you were in?' I ask.

'For sure. He still trading shots of Phegia for blowjobs?'

'Oh yeah,' I say. 'He'll be under report any day now, half the babes in the teen dorms are junkified to the max.'

'Fugging dickbag,' he says.

I flash him a coy little sidesmile as someone else asks me something and he sits back against the wall, folding his hands up behind his head, coysmiling right back.

I'm totally throwing this one down later on.

One of the kids who came on the bus with me sits on my seat with his pillow between us.

'Saw that dog Uncle gag you on the ride in,' he says, and throws me a fist bump. I bump him back and shake my head.

'Gotta get a hold of my mouth, I'm up for Age Release in a week and I have a strike against me already.'

'What happens if you get two more strikes?' asks a little twelver two pillows over.

'For strikes they can put me into detention for up to a month after I turn eighteen. So just late release. But if I commit one of the five deadly sins . . .'

'Right to a Prisoncorp,' says Blondie and I nod. Everyone kinda looks down for a bit. Verity House and all the other Orphancorps (Sunshine Gardens, KidsCo, and the most ruthless and diabolical of all, Punkin Patch) buy unaccompanied minors from the state and can't keep 'em past eighteen. That is, unless they mess up, then it's right to a Prisoncorp. Once you're in there, it's pretty much the end of it.

'So, you got any skills?' asks a South Asian kid about my age with long, silky black hair. I can't tell if they're male or female, but it doesn't matter because sweet babes need no gender.

I pull up my sleeves and the hem of my nightshirt.

'I tattoo. No machine, just stick and poke.'

All the kids ooh and ahh over the blue-black designs that twist and dance all over my skin. 'You have to be over fifteen though, and if they see the tats and want you to spill, you don't know me, yeah?'

'Of course,' says Blondie and I'm hoping he wants some kind of complicated lower ab piece 'cause I'd be really into that.

'What about you guys?' I ask.

'I make a pretty good corn wine,' Blondie says.

'Toilet?' I ask.

'No way. Got batches going up in the roofs here and there. I can also get you some weed if that's your thing.'

Of course. Gardeners can always get you weed.

The S.A. cutie flicks their long 'do back over one shoulder.

'I'm Ara. I work in the metalshop and I can make all kinds of stuff. Keys and tools or whatever you need. No weapons though, I'm a lover, not a fighter.' Their name and voice are just as androgynous as the rest of them. I shake a delicate, long-fingered hand.

'I'm a doc,' says a stone-face girl with fierce grey eyes and acne-spotted cheeks. 'No-snitch stitches, tooth-yanking, terminations, that sort of stuff.'

There's the usual assortment of black market traders and pill-shillers, and one nondescript boy with wild, black-circled eyes who tells me he will cop the blame for an infraction and even do a stint in Time Out for the right kinda trade. Fugging weirdo. We've moved onto a rundown on the general attitudes, tempera-ments and suspected menstrual cycles of the Uncles and Aunties when Aunt Bev throws open the door.

'You little shits need to keep it down, the bubs are trying to sleep.' Behind her I can hear a toddler wailing.

'Do ya think the crying might have something to do with the harsh realities of the conditions we live under, and not our pretty tame and quiet convo, Aunt Bev?' I ask her and all the kids snicker. She doesn't have her tab on her so I don't get a mark down but she gives me a withering look and we get into bed before she storms in and starts making a scene.

Kids are settling in, deep-breathing, sleep-farting and starting to snore when I see a shadow break the moonlight and spill over my bed.

'So, I was thinking of having you do a tat for me, but I'm not sure where,' whispers Blondie. I lift up my sheet and he slides in beside me.

'Wanna take a look at some of mine?' I ask and he pulls my nightshirt up over my head. 'It might give you some ideas.'

'I like this one,' he says, lifting my arms above my head and nipping at a little design on my bicep before burying his nose in my armpit hair. I twist my head to one side and stare at the thin ink lines. It's an image of a flower I found in the playground once. Blondie smells like earth and sweat and sunshine. He works his way down between my legs and pulls at my underpants with his teeth.

'So, I'm Mirii,' I say, and he comes back up and kisses my mouth.

'I'm Ben.'

'I'm going to call you Blondie,' I say, and he laughs. I roll him over and run my tongue all the way down his side. 'I think this is a good place for a tattoo.' I nibble at his hip and I can tell that he agrees.

—

After Blondie leaves I curl up under the sweat-soggy

sheet. The thrum in my body almost drowns out the quiet night-sobbing in the littlies dorm next door, but then there's a great clatter-crash that jolts me up out of bed. It sets off the babies down the hall, which is just fugging great.

'Catch her, Mahoney!'

At my name, I jump up and before I know what I'm aiming for, I raise my hands and grab, getting handfuls of greasy hair. The lights come on and I see my hands are sunk into long, white-blonde strands attached to an oval-shaped face with green eyes flashing hate and glee and a mouth missing the right canine tooth.

'Please,' Freya says.

'Sorry babe, gotta do what the man says,' I say, and wrangle her into a good headlock until the Uncles catch up, puffing. Even though she's down and I've got a tight hold, they still taze her. She stiffens and tips over and the kiddie-prod catches me too as we topple towards the ground, zapping me right on the shoulder. All the parts of me go rigid and my teeth sink tight into the very tip of my tongue as the bolts peal around my body. When the pain subsides, I can feel I've pissed myself. The urine and the blood from my tooth-gouged tongue mix in a puddle on the floor as I shuddershuddershudder. Rage and voltage zing through me. I'm seeing stars.

'On your feet, Freeman.' Freya untangles her limbs

from mine and stands unsteadily. They prod her, make her stand again. This game goes on until it's not fun for them any more, then one of the Uncles twists her arm up behind her back and they march off. She looks down at me and mouths something that looks like 'truck you' but probably isn't, but then she smiles her marred smile for a moment before she disappears. For some reason, lying in a puddle of my own assortment of liquids, I smile too.

—

I don't know if it's the prodding that shakes me up so hard, but while I lie in the dark and try to breathe my way through the fizzy jump of all my muscles and nerves, I start to think about my mum and dad.

The lady who I reckon was my mum had really nice brown skin and dark eyes and wavy brown hair that went all the way down her back. I think I can remember the tickle of her hair on my face as she looked down on me. The dad, he had orange hair and a red nose and kind green eyes. I mean, I'm not sure if they even are my mum and dad because of the whole thing about how I must have been just a little dumbshiz kid when I came into the corp and all I have are these random memory flashes, but I reckon they are. I look like an even mash of the two of them: his green eyes and her brown skin and hair that's a weird mix of the two, brown and wavy, run through with threads of copper.

But too, I know they must be special because of something in the way they looked at me, yeah? Like I was theirs and they'd made me and they loved me just heaps and stuff.

I'm glad I've got that to hang onto. Most of the kids here don't. It helps to know that somewhere, sometime, a couple of folks loved me, even if it was only for a little while.

SIX DAYS

'What's that?' the little kid asks, pointing to the tattoo peeking out of my sleeve.

'Nothing. Bugger off,' I say, brushing him away like a fly and just like a fly, he buzzes back in.

'Is it a tattoo? Can I see?' he asks.

I huff and blow my hair out of my eyes, focusing in on the headset I'm wiring up. It's fiddly work and this kid's got me distracted. My hands are covered in little white circle-scars from drips of liquid hot solder and I'm not looking to add another right now.

'It's nothing. Now, piss off, kid.' I roll my sleeve down so he stops asking.

I hate kids. I think I even hated kids back when I was one and I try my very best to avoid them, which is no easy feat when you live in fugging Orphancorp.

The little dropkick is a runner for my section and I don't want to get him talking to me so whenever I need something I get up and get it myself, which of course makes the Auntie in charge of my section suspicious.

'Mahoney, next time I see you get up out of that seat, I'm going to put my boot so far up your bum you'll be able to see the tread on your tongue.'

'That's a good one, Auntie,' I tell her. 'I'm gunna use that.'

'My pleasure, Mahoney. I do it all for you.' She pulls out a tab and lifts one finger to the screen. 'Now, do I have to write you up, or are you going to sit down?'

I park my arse. 'I'm down.'

She gestures to the kid. 'Get this little kicker to get your wires or pliers or whatever.'

He grins. He's about eleven, a real goofy-looking kid with big ears, and a wide, tanned and freckled face.

'What's your name, fuggface?'

'Cam.'

'Right, Cam, I need a pair of needlenose pliers,' I start and the little brownnoser takes right off but I grab him by the sleeve of his grubby lemon-yellow shirt and pull him back. He's so skinny and insubstantial that I almost reef him right off the ground as he swings back towards me.

'But, I don't want any shizzy, busted up pair. No rust. No solder gumming up everything. And the grips need to be intact, no tears. If you're gonna run for me, you don't bring me any poor quality tools, got it?'

He nods, big dumb smile on his doofus face. He runs off to the supply shed and the joke's on him 'cause I've got the last pair of good pliers right there on my workstation, but at least this way he'll be digging through the tools 'til lunch break and that gives me a bunch of time to find another timewaster job to keep him out of my hair 'til knockoff time.

———

The toilets are in a line in the bathroom, no cubicles or doors because, fuggit, that would give us some dignity or something. For once the entire bathroom is empty until the door opens and someone comes in. It's that Freya chick from yesterday. I lower my eyes, because it's the thing to do in the bathrooms and besides, I'm halfway through the most epic piss and don't feel like making eye contact with some biatch-stranger I barely know while I void the three-hour-bladder I've had brewing all morning.

I'm watching a roach skitter out from behind the loo and run between my boots when I hear the thud of footsteps and I look up. Freya's skipping towards me and in her hand flashes something sharp and deadly-looking. Sick hot fear slices through me 'cause there's this emptiness in her gleamy green eyes and I jump up, staining my pants with a dark splatter of pee.

'You hurt me last night,' she hisses, jamming her hard, thin body against me, arm circling my neck like the headlock I had her in last night. Her hipbones drive

into the base of my spine and her tiny breasts mash under my shoulder blades. She pulls me back down onto the toilet and wraps her legs tight around my waist, squeezing 'til my ribs scream.

'Dontcha age out in a few days? Dontcha think you should be more careful?' Freya asks. I feel the sharp edge of whatever she's holding dig into my cheek.

'I'm really sorry, Freya,' I say, breathing hard against her crushing thighs and the wiry arm across my neck. 'But you would have done the same as me.'

'Bugger off I would have,' she says.

'Bullshiz. When the man tells you to jump, you ask them if they'd like sugar on top.'

'Fuck the man,' Freya says, like a petulant little kid.

'Yeah maybe, but babe, I don't know you. I'm not risking my release for no one, let alone some fugging stranger.'

'What kind of attitude is that?'

'The kind of attitude than means I'll get out of here and have a chance at a real life.'

'You won't.' She collapses a little bit against me. The sharp point pulls away and the sting eases. Then she takes a big breath and goes rigid again and the knife digs in and this time I feel hot blood spill down my face and drip onto the floor. My face is on fire as she drags the spike against my cheek and my nerves scream as the flesh splits apart but I stay silent.

This is the second time I've spilled my own blood

and piss onto the floor since I got here and both times have had a lot to do with this Freya chick. I wonder how much more I'm going to spill in the next week because of her.

———

The grey-eyed girl, Nerida, breathes sour breath into my face. She's one of those girls who looks right into you and so I look anywhere but into her black-flecked irises. I settle on a nasty looking, pus-filled volcano-zit by her nose. My fingers claw up as she catches the edge of the wound with the fine, curved needle and sinks it in.

'Fuggit! Don't you have any local or anything? What kind of doc are you?'

She lets go of the needle. I can see it, out of the corner of my eye, hanging out of my cheek.

'Do you want me to do this or not? The infirmary is right around the corner, and I'm pretty sure they won't use a local, and they'll probably slam you in the pokey as well, if you don't tell them who did it.'

'Okay, okay. It just stings, that's all. Got any corn wine? Potato punch?'

'No. Now please shut up and stay fugging still.' Nerida leans back in and I feel the needle pull through the skin and I gasp as it bites into the other side. Little zigs and zags of pain shoot through all the nerves on my face and I pant as she draws the split skin together and ties the thread off with a practiced flourish. Then the needle dives in again and I draw a sharp breath and grip hard onto the sink.

We're in the dorm bathroom and there's a little just-teen outside on watch so none of the Aunties come waddling in to bust us down to Time Out. It's lunch hour, so the dorms are deserted, but you can't be too careful.

'So Freya's mad that you turned her in the other night?'

'Yeah, I guess,' I say, wincing and trying not to move my mouth too much. 'I don't know, it seems like overkill, yeah? What was I supposed to do, say "nah"?'

'Freya doesn't think like that,' Nerida says, and ties off again, diving back into my screaming skin without even a pause to catch my breath.

'Does she have a thing with Blondie Ben the gardener? I may have had a bit of cuddle time with him last night.'

'Ben's good like that,' she says, and is that a hint of wist I detect? 'Nah, that would be too easy. She doesn't care about stuff like that. She's new. She was living wild out in the Western Suburbs until a year or so ago. I don't know how they caught her, but she's not like us. She doesn't get how it works. She's not, like, broken yet.'

Nerida digs in again and I clench my teeth. 'Last one, Mirii.'

'Thank fugg.'

'She's been here about three months and she's spent half that time in Time Out. She's even done a stint in the Naughty Chair. We thought that one might finally break her, but it's like it's just made her even more mad.' She pulls the last stitch together gently and I groan as she knots it. 'There, all done.'

I lie back against the tiles, the whole right side of my face thumping.

'I don't want a tattoo for the trade, but I know Ara Jadhav wants one and they've got what I want, so talk to them later.' She goes over to the sink and washes her hands. 'The kid we've got on watch for us? You owe her your fruit from dinner tonight. Don't forget, because she won't.'

'What do *you* want?' I ask her, but she just slams her little med bag closed.

'None of ya business.'

'Right-o then.' I'm in no mood to probe. She walks off without looking back and I take a few seconds to breathe through the pain, then I slam it back to the buzz shop because lunch break's almost over.

—

'Mahoney, what's that on your face?' The Uncle on watch in the buzz shop peers at my cheek, his forehead all crunched up above his big red honker nose. I can smell the booze coming off him in waves.

'Nothing, Uncle Jeff.'

'They look like stitches.'

'You're an observant old bastard, aren't you?'

'You're a mouthy little bitch, aren't you?' he says and he comes towards me. With that kind of tone I know better than to sass him back, and I shrink into myself as much as I can. See, I was thinking daffy-drunk-Uncle, when he's really aggressive-boozed-up-dude-in-power. My mistake.

'Sorry Uncle Jeff.' I put on my best beaten-dog look. If I had a tail it would be between my legs. Angry old jerks like him dig that submissive vibe. 'I got these back at Orange. Had an accident on the playground.'

'You run your mouth like that again and you'll be having another accident pretty soon.'

I nod and skitter back to my workstation before I piss him off any further. I add him to the shiz-list I've got in my head under the subheading of 'angry drunk arseholes'.

Cam comes up and puts a shiny-looking pair of pliers on the table. He looks up at me with a big, dumb grin on his dork face, like he can't believe what an impressive fugg he is for pulling this gleamy, almost-new tool from some magical tool-stash in the ether, but then the smile crumbles away.

'Wow, Mirii. What happened?'

'Nothing.' I say, trying to strip a piece of wire, the

most basic of tasks that I'd even trust this jerk to do, and snapping it instead. My hands still tremble and Cam sees it and takes the stuff from me, stripping the plastic sheaths from the wires with surprisingly tricky fingers. He hands them back to me and I take a few deep breaths to steady myself.

'So, what's with the tattoos?' he asks, tapping my arm a few times for emphasis.

'I don't know. What's with your face?' I finish the delicate loop and twist of the wires and I don't even have to reach for the cover, because Cam is right there, handing it to me already.

'How come you have so many?'

''Cause I can. 'Cause they can't make me wash 'em off.'

The kid nods. He gets it. I smile, even though it stings like a bitch, and hand him the finished headset. He wraps it in a plastic cover, drops it in the box and starts gathering up parts for the next one.

I pull my sleeve higher and trace the inked pattern on my arm, six diamonds linked by a thin black line, remembering the midnight grey night I poked it; the heat of the needle, the sting of the ink.

'What is it?'

'This one? It's a constellation. That's a pattern of stars. It's in the shape of a boat. It's called Carina.' The talking hurts my face, but it helps to relax me a little bit. Helps me push Freya's mean green eyes away.

'Like the stars in the sky? Why'd you put them on you?'

'Why you ask so many questions?'

He shrugs.

'Okay, you ever been in a corp out in the desert?' I ask. 'Like out Bourke way? At night the stars are everywhere, not like here in the city where you can't see them at all. I looked them up on the net and it turns out the stars are how people used to find their way around before sats or even maps. They'd make the patterns in the sky to guide their way home. I liked the idea of being able to find my way around.'

'But how?'

'I guess they'd just look up and search for the patterns, yeah? Then follow them. Like, the first people who lived here, way back thousands of years ago.'

'The abbos?'

'Don't say that, that's a derogatory word.'

'What's dirogory?'

'Derogatory. It's like a mean word, a hate word. Don't say it. They're called Aboriginals. Or like, Indigenous.'

'Shiz, sorry,' he says, and his cheeks flush a mean shade of red that spreads out all the way to his batwing ears. 'I don't hate Aboriginals or nothing.'

'It's cool, just don't say that word no more. Anyway, they'd make up stories about the shapes in the stars and tell the stories to each other so everyone knew how to find home.'

'Are you an indigenous? Your skin is pretty brown.'

'I think so. My name, Miriiyanan, means shooting star in an Aboriginal language. Gamilaraay. I looked it up.'

'You know a bunch of stuff, huh?'

I nod.

'Do you go to school?' he asks.

'Yeah. Do you?' I raise my eyebrow and glare at him because too few kids do and it's a real shame.

'Nah. Too tired in the mornings.' He looks sheepish and he takes the box even though it's only three-quarters full and heads off down between the rows of workstations, weaving through the spotlit buzzshop islands 'til I lose him in the flow.

———

'I know who did that to your face,' says a husky girlvoice. The speaker slots herself in next to me. 'Vu, Adeline,' she says, and offers a fist. 'Call me Vu though, everyone does.'

'Mahoney. Miriiyanan. Mirii,' I say and bump her. She pulls her fist back and spreads her fingers out, like they're exploding in slo-mo. It's an inner-city thing. Vu has long dark hair on two-thirds of her head, with the rest scraped to the scalp. She wears a pair of too-big, ultra thick glasses and a dirty pale-orange shirt with darker orange sweat-stains in the pits and the buttons close to bursting across her chest.

'Was it Freya? It was her, right?' Vu asks. There's a twisted knot of scar tissue on her right cheek too.

'Was *that* Freya?' I ask, nodding towards the puckered skin.

'Sure was, when we were both at the Engadine house. She thought I dobbed on her to the guards.'

'Did you?'

'Totally didn't, not that time anyway. I did every chance I could afterward, though. I figure I earned it.'

'What's it to you, anyway?'

'Well, if it was Freya —'

'It might have been,' I say.

'Then we have something in common.' She dips a meat nugget into the squirt of brown-flavoured sauce on her tray, then shoves the whole thing in her mouth. I nibble at mine. A bunch of kids who seem to know and love Vu come and sit with us.

'Is everyone here cool?' I whisper to Vu.

'Yeah,' she says, spitting little bits of mystery meat and breading on my arm. I wipe it off as she gestures to a prissy-looking chick sitting near the door. 'You have to watch out for Kelly Karmine, she's getting it on with Uncle Dereck.' She nods towards a young, beefy and neckless Uncle standing on duty by the door. He keeps sneaking looks over at Karmine and it's pretty obvious and gross.

'Kelly's got a loose mouth, among other things.

Everyone else from the teen dorm is okay, unless they're in the Naughty Chair, but who can keep their mouth shut there, really?'

'Cool.' I raise my voice to be heard by the rest of the table. 'So, who do I see about keys? I got a mish I need to do tonight.'

A tall, thin guy waves a hand. He's got a little 'fro going and tribal scars on his cheeks. 'I'm your man. Ade.'

I reach over and we bump. 'You need a toll?'

'Nah, sister. Danger is my reward.'

'Ah, a man after my own heart.'

Ara slots in across from me, shaking out their long hair so they don't sit on it.

'Hey, Ara?'

They raise a finely-shaped eyebrow at me.

'Nerida said you have something she wants. I gotta pay her for these stitches,' I say, waving at the tight, sore part of my face. 'She said you might want what I've got going.'

Ara rolls their eyes. 'Bloody Nerida. She's right, but. Can you do names?' Their voice is weird and low and kinda skips a bit when they say 'names'.

'Of course.'

'Good,' Ara says. 'I'm down to trade.'

—

'Don't you have, like, a week left until you go?' Vu asks. She presses up against me by the door and she smells like sweet sweat and like mandarins, which we got with our dinner tonight. Apparently she was owed fruit for something because she had a bunch of them and she peeled and ate them one by one as the kids told stories before tuck in. She didn't share with anyone else, but she gave a few of the little crescents to me. That meant something, but I'm not sure what.

'Five days tomorrow.'

'Then why are you going on a mish? Do you want to get caught or something?'

'Of course I don't, don't be stupid.' I say and I guess it's true, but I wonder . . .

'Most kids with as much time as you left keep their heads down and do the time. They don't go out on missions and they don't pick fights with unpredictable bitches *and* they don't backtalk to the A and U's.'

'I like living on the edge,' I say and grin at her, but it's all for show and I reckon she knows it. Inside I'm really wondering the same thing.

Like, I thought when I was almost there I'd chill out, but if anything, I've got worse. Kids always talk about Age Transfer with such gravity, like it's some golden time and they've got this big, gaping freedom coming up, and it's like that but it's also not. Freedom feels scary, feels too big and every time I think about what I might do I stop being able to think about anything.

'Mirii. Mirii! Mahoney, are you in there?' Vu asks, knocking on my head.

'Shiz, yes. Yes.'

'I don't think you're up for a mish, babe. You just voided out like, whoa. You been smoking up with Farmer Ben?'

'I wish,' I say. 'I gotta go out, Vu. I need gloves and alcohol wipes, gotta make some trade. I owe for these stitches. If you're worried, then stay here.'

'Nah, I wanna come. I haven't been on a mish in ages. I need some excitement. Do you get mad toey and hungry afterwards?'

'Who doesn't?' I say, then hush her. Auntie Carol's on nightwatch and the girl at the workstation next to mine said that she always gets into the med supply cupboard and dopes out on Calmucet or Tarmiene. Perfect mish conditions. Through the grill on the door I can see her take a seat behind the watch station and within thirty seconds she's already on the nod.

'Time?' Vu breathes into my ear and it tickles: my ear and elsewhere. I brush her back a little, but she shoves herself up against me again.

'Nearly.'

Auntie Carol's head drops again, comes up. Drops, up again. Drops, drops, drops . . . She lets out a big, honking snore.

'Let's kick this baby,' I breathe and I open the door extra-slow and careful-like. Vu follows tight-close behind me and we whisper across the scuffed, moonlit linoleum in bare feet. I've got the key ring clamped tight in my hand so it doesn't jingle but I reckon I could stomp double time across the floor, shaking the keys like a tambourine, popping out cartwheels and singing the national anthem at the top of my lungs and Carol would keep napping through the whole thing. She's pretty gone.

Vu and I skitter into the watch station. She keeps an eye out while I slam a flash bead into the Systower. It's this mean little patch that I scored off a kid back out at the Lightning Ridge house when I was a little thirteen-year-old scumbag. He was this hack-genius and the patch runs a stealth prog that kinda pauses all the cameras but keeps the timers running so it looks like nothing's happening. I mean, half the kidcams don't even work, but better safe than sorry, yeah? Cost me a month's fruit and I ended up with bleeding gums but it's paid for itself about ten times over and it's never let me down. That or none of the cameras work. Either way.

That prog has spread through the Orphancorps like herpes through a teen dorm, and there's a bunch of copies floating around now. Standard issue for a mish, but I get off on using my old orig copy. Like retro hipster chic, yeah? I had it before it was cool.

'We're good to go?' Vu says and when I nod she pops her head back in the dorm and a few other kids run out and scatter down the hall on their own missions.

Me and Vu skip towards the Sick Bay. I do pop out a cartwheel now, 'cause I'm extra jolted to be out in the wee hours and it feels cool to have Vu padding down the hallway beside me, her hair and nightshirt rippling.

Sick Bay door opens with a massive crunch of the lock that has me wincing, but no rogue night-time Auntie or Uncle comes to check out the noise so we pop the door open and slink into the infirmary. I go right for the supply cupboard, snatching up a whole box of alcohol wipes because there's ten of them in there, then I empty the box of small surgical gloves halfway and muddle the rest around to disguise the missing bulk. Vu goes to the pharm supply cupboard and I throw her the keys. She pops the lock, takes a few Tarmienes from a bottle on the top shelf, but not too many because Auntie Carol's already piggied up a bunch of them tonight and she doesn't want it to be too obvs. Then she pockets a preloaded syringe of Calmucet and I'm like, not as cool with that.

'You into heavy shit, hey? Your arms look okay, I didn't think you jabbed. You a groiner? In between the toes?'

'It's not for me, it's for trade. I owe big.'

'Looks like. What did you do?'

'Got knocked up last month. Needed some of Nerida's special tea.'

'Oh, sorry. You okay?'

'I was once it was gone, right?' She lets out a big laugh, like, 'Ha!' and then claps a hand over her mouth.

'What does Nerida want the Calmucet for?'

'She's the jabber.'

'Wow. I didn't know.'

'It's not like she sings it from the tabletops at dinnertime.'

'Guess not.'

Vu pops the stuff into her bra and smooths her nightie over the lumps. 'So, you wanna go down to the admin offices and jimmy some of the Aunties' and Uncles' lockers? They've always got lollies and shit. We could be high-rolling traders for the rest of the week.'

'Sure, why not?'

I close the Sick Bay door behind me and pull it twice to make sure it's locked. Then Vu grabs me round the waist and we dance down towards the admin office by the front door, our night shirts flying up, bright in the moonlight. She dips me right by the door and I slide the key in while I'm upside down. She pulls me up, spins me and I push the door open with my foot.

There's a light on inside.

—

The light is a bright strip under the door to the Warden's office. Vu and I pause mid-breath, still cheek-to-cheek from our impromptu dance-number.

'Vile,' she breathes. She's still gripping one of my hands and she drops my waist and pulls me away. The door creaks as it closes. We race back up the hall.

'You're right,' I whisper as we pass the infirmary. 'Totally gross. What a waste.'

'Not gross,' she says. 'Vile. Warden Vile. Warden Kyle, I don't know what he's doing here, but if he sees us we're up the scheisse creek.'

'Paddle?'

'Yeah, nah,' she says, extra-grim.

And it's then that I hear the footsteps bouncing off the walls. Hard soled shoes. Squeaky.

Warden shoes.

My heart speeds up and my guts turn to water, start to churn like someone's pressed my flush button. Vu and I swing it past the nursery dorms and I make a quick eye contact with a night Nanny who happens to be peering out of the window. I press a finger to my mouth but I'm going too fast to see if she nods or not.

I'm pretty sure a bunch of kids are raiding the kitchen or up in one of the workshops on a light-finger mish but there's no time to warn them. We power past Auntie Carol who's drooling all over herself with her chin resting on her chest and her feet up on the countertop.

Vu opens the door real swift and quiet and I fly in behind her, skidding around to lock the door up tight. Ade's sitting up and I sling the keys to him across the bunkbed forest of snoring teeners. He catches them fast in one hand as I dive for my bed. In the hallway there's a shout and a yelp and a clatter as this Warden dude lays one out on Auntie Carol, busted asleep at the wheel. I wriggle further down under the covers and try to slow my heartbeat from a mad voidstep thump to something more ambient. The lock grinds, deafening and slow and then the door opens.

'Up. All of you up! Now. Stand next to your bunks.'

The lights go on and everyone's already up, blinking in the hum of fluorescence.

The Warden is a squat, portly fugger with slick black hair, a sharp, dark suit and a button-up shirt that's the cleanest, whitest thing I've ever seen. His tie chokes him tight under his loose, shaven neck.

'Five missing from their beds, Carol. Who are they?'

'I'm, um, I'm . . .' Carol slurs. She's probably in as much shit as we are, if not more.

'Get out, Carol. Call the watch down from the tower, then wait in my office.'

Carol shuffles off, tripping on a crack in the linoleum, mumbling and crying to herself.

Warden Vile paces through the rows of mattresses, tapping something in the palm of his hand. He does it on purpose, to slam up the tension. He's quiet and we're quiet and the air's all zappy like just before a storm. He passes by me, so close that if I lifted my hand just a little, it would brush across the fine stuff his suit's made of. What are suits made of? It looks itchy. I wonder if he can feel my heart trip-hopping under my ribs, smell the fear-sweat trickling out from under my arms.

He looks right at me. I've got at least twenty centimetres height-wise on him and it feels weird and wrong to be looking down at this man because his presence feels so mighty. I feel like I should lay flat on the floor to show him that I know my place. Show him that I know he could end me at any second if I so much as breathed wrong.

Then I stop breathing. Everything goes slow and liquid. I can feel my face desaturate. My legs cramp and my fingers turn to stone.

That thing he's tap-tap-tapping in his palm? It's my flash bead. My patch. I left it in the Systower and if he finds out it's mine, I'm crumpets.

FIVE DAYS

Vile points to a blinking, half-asleep kid with wild bedhead.

'You. Who is missing from their beds?'

The kid doesn't hesitate for a second. None of us would, not when it's this obvious. If he asked Freya right now, even she'd spill like a knocked-over cup.

'Belham. Hough. Chen. Smith, Clover Smith. And . . . I think that's Jadhav's?' he says, twisting up a brow, trying to remember.

Ara puts their hand up. 'I'm Jadhav. That mattress is Cook's.'

'Right,' the cyclone-haired kid says. 'Yeah, Praz Cook sleeps there. Sorry Ara.'

'Good,' Vile says. He still taps the flash bead in his palm. His hands are white and pink, soft like flower petals. The nails gleam like shiny plastic. He keeps up his pacing round the mattresses and every eye in the room darts from place to place, following his course.

'And who knows what this is?' He holds up the flash

bead. From here it's just a tiny black dot between his thumb and forefinger, but we all raise our hands. He points to the closest girl.

'It's a flash bead.'

'Yes. And who does it belong to?'

No hands. The silence is long. The buzz of the light fills up all the spaces in between us. I see a slight dip of a white-blonde head by the window. Freya. I look at her. She looks at me. She raises an eyebrow and her eyes gleam with knowledge. They're asking me, *should I?* I try and make my face say, *don't you fugging dare, you twisted bitch*, but that's a lot for one expression to say and I don't know if my message is that loud *or* clear.

The door slams inwards and every kid in the room jumps half a foot. I jolt in the heart and in the guts and it feels like my blood starts running backwards. A bunch of the Aunties and Uncles from the night watches and up in the tower trot in, proud as pie, with all the mish kids by the collars. They look defeated as shiz.

'Take those children right down to the Consequence wing.'

Everyone winces, though I don't know why we expected different. It's not like they woulda tucked 'em back into bed. They march out and Vile gives us a cold once-over with those deep black eyes before he sweeps out. The door locks and the lights go out with a crump. I blink against the dark, blind in the absence of the sick white light and climb back under the covers. When I can see again I look over at Vu who looks over at me, her face heavy like a storm cloud. She crawls over and I lift the blankets for her. Cuddling up against me, I feel her body start to shake.

'If it wasn't . . . If we didn't . . .'

'I know. I know, Vu. This is our fault too and if they zing us to the man, we'll cop. If they don't . . . I don't know. We'll find some way to make it up to them.'

I let her tears soak into my nightie and when she's done crying, Vu pulls me hard to her and her tongue is in my mouth and she rakes her fingernails across my back. I know what she wants. I can feel the ripple of scar tissue in lines across her thighs. I catch glimpses of the long-healed, and less-healed slashes on her arms in the silver moonlight. I sink my hands into her hair, twist it up between my fingers and yank it back hard. She lets her head go and I follow her back with my teeth at her neck. She breathes sharp and presses herself tight against my hipbone.

Sometimes here the hurt and the good feelings get all mixed up. Sometimes they become the same thing. And sometimes you gotta feel your way out of the pain in your brain. There are lots of ways to do it.

This is one.

—

After, when Vu is curled into my side, exhausted and deep asleep and I'm laying there, eyes closed and mind racing, I feel . . . something. A presence. I open my eyes and Freya's standing there, inverted in my vision — legs-body-head-pale-hair — above the mattress. Her grey nightdress and hair glow in the dark but the bruises on her face make it into a void. She doesn't say anything, but then again, she doesn't need to.

—

It takes me three tries to plug in my tab in the purple morning light and I nod my way through two lessons on the free-school site until I give up and lay my head down on the desk for a bit before work starts.

It's still and quiet with only the low thump of a few fingers on tab screens, but I can't sleep because I can't stop the circles in my mind. I see the faces of the kids who got caught out of bed, a flash of the door to the Consequence wing, Freya's missing tooth, Warden Kyle's cold grey eyes. The classroom has bright lemon-yellow walls and an ancient whiteboard scrawled with the ghosts of old marker. There's a much-scrubbed but still not-gone epitaph of the word 'balls' in giant letters from the top to the bottom and I stare hard at it to escape the visions in my mind, trying to solidify the ghost-words. One of the lights in the left corner flickers and strobes across the gleaming whiteboard.

The dodgy light is a sign. When I get into the buzzshop Uncle Jeff sends me and Cam, who's unofficially appointed himself my personal runner, plus another buzzy and his runner over to the dorms to replace the wiring on some of the overhead lights. It's feeding time in the nursery and we peer into the zoo, get a glimpse of the mad, scrambling battle-royale of tots for their bots, get a whiff of the stink of milk-spew.

'The Four-to-Seven dorm first, yeah?' the other Buzzer, Gregor, asks me and I nod like mad.

'For sure.'

They've cleared off an area under the fixture, roped it off with some yellow and black checker-tape and opened up a rickety ladder. Gregor and I Fist-Peace-Faceplant to see who goes up first (fist beats peace, peace revives a faceplant, faceplant flops all over a fist) and I win. Cam and the other runner, Sticksy, hold the ladder while Gregor climbs up to suss out the sitch and I get busy laying out all the tools we might need.

While I'm digging through the rusty toolbox, I eavesdrop on a tight group of scummy tykes nearby. The boss of this gathering is a girl of about six with a runny nose and a long tangle of ashy-blonde hair. She sits in the middle of an arc of rapt kids, telling a story in a loud, nasal voice to be heard over the shrieks and giggles of a hundred other little jerks.

'. . . they eat the light, and drink the noise the lights make. That buzz sound. They eat it all up.'

She's talking about the grey ones. That's what we used to call them, but it changes. It always changes.

'I never seen no grey ghosts,' says a boy about her age. She throws him a look of pure malice, the way only a six-year-old can.

'That's because you're gunna die soon,' she tells him, pure and matter-of-fact. 'You can't see them if you gunna die soon. Then you'll be one of 'em.'

The little boy goes a pale green colour. He turns to a wide-eyed dribbler with a shocking bowl-cut next to him, punches him in the stomach, and storms off through the room.

Tangles takes the crying kid into her arms and rocks him 'til he shuts up. She sucks a noseful of snot back into her nostrils and continues.

'Grey ghosts come from all the kids who die here. They can't hurt you, but. They just can't ever die proper because they don't got no family to let them into heaven. You gotta know people in there to get in.'

The mouth-breathers sit there and nod.

'In the day time they live in the lights, eating and drinking lots. Then at night they come out and play in the hallways and in the stairwell down to the con-sa-kents wing, but they don't play fun games. They have to play hidey-findey all night and not ever find each other. Just look and look forever.'

'Can they see each other?' asks a tiny little golden-skinned boy with tight ringlets spilling over his brow and a rippled burn scar on his neck.

'Nope. There's lots of 'em but they feel like they're all alone.'

'Oh,' the kids chorus.

That's new, I haven't heard that one before. I reckon Tangles made it up on the spot. These stories get passed around like rumours and gossip, changing that little bit with every telling, but the base is always the same.

Tangles drops her voice to a loud whisper. 'That big girl and the boy up on the ladder, they're tryna help. She's got special tools to try and get the ghosts out of the lights and send them to heaven.'

The kids sneakily peer over at me and I look up and wink. Some of the real little ones gasp.

Fugg me, kids are stupid.

—

I'm up the ladder in the nursery, getting twisted in loose wire when I glance down and see Vu looking up at me. She's got a bub on her hip, winding its hand in her thick black hair.

'Hey Mirii,' she says. Her eyes are puffy and dark-circled and there's a row of little marks on her neck. Those are mine and seeing them runs electricity through me, but not real current because the power's been switched off in here. Like, the metaphorical kind, yeah?

'Hey Vu, I didn't know you worked the nursery.'

'Yeah, I've been on this detail for four months, since my last transfer,' she says, bouncing the tiny blob. It waves its grubby little hands around, grins and lets out a laugh that even I think is cute. Then it opens its mouth and a big glug of white vomit comes out and goes down the front of Vu's lavender top.

'The spew smell never comes out. Did my hair reek of it last night?' She grins up at me.

'I didn't notice,' I say, coysmiling right back.

She hands the kid off to another Nanny and uses the threadbare towel over her shoulder to mop up the mess on her shirt. There are heaps of older kids in here working Nanny detail. Apparently, if bubs don't get a bunch of attention and stuff when their gooey brains are growing, they end up useless and kinda crazy. Orphancorps need workers, not angry kids that prefer rocking back and forth over working in the factories, so they put a bunch of the older kids on Nanny detail. I wonder how long it took them to figure that out? Some of the kids are hopeless on daycare duty, but some of them are good at giving out the love and stuff. Not me, though. I did it once for a few months and it sucked the life right out of me. Kids are such little balls of need, aren't they?

'So, I heard from Bates this morning, he was on mop-up down in Consequences,' Vu says, popping a pacifier back in the mouth of some kid who spat it out. 'He said it was a pretty deep cleanup scene but that everyone's in Time Out now. A couple of them went through the corner and the chair in the wee hours, but it don't look like they're gonna spill. I think if they had we'd be toast already.'

'Makes sense, yeah. Still have those Calmucets from last night?'

She nods yes.

'Maybe we can trade 'em and get the kitchens to send some decent food down?'

Vu nods and folds her arms around herself. 'It's the least we can do. I wish we could do more.'

'Me too.'

From over in the corner there's a clatter and a scream. A blobber's toppled over or something and bashed a whole row of them down like dominoes. My jaw tightens as the room erupts in screams.

'I don't know if I could do this job,' I say, stepping carefully down the ladder as Cam and Sticksy hold it tight.

'I actually don't mind it. You stop hearing the noise after a while. I like working with the real little ones the most of all.'

We watch as Cam and Sticks try and settle the unrest by starting a game of Zoom. Soon the bubs are all giggling and clapping their hands like they're having the time of their blobby little lives.

'Real little bubs are easy, ya know?' Vu says. 'There's only, like four things they want. Food, to be changed, to sleep or a cuddle. That's about it. I like that.'

'If only all people were so easy.'

'Right?' she says.

———

'I want you to do a tattoo on me,' Cam says, watching as I wire up another headset, then another and another.

It's hell-hot in the buzzshop and everyone pauses now and then to mop up sweat, roll out their ankles and stretch out kinks in tight necks and shoulders. At this point in the day everyone's hit a good rhythm and we pick, prod, solder, sleeve and pack like we're manufactured for it, like we're windup. Cam hands me tools before I even know I need them. I guess he's okay, but that doesn't mean I'd break my rules for him.

'You're not old enough for a tattoo,' I tell him.

'Am too!'

I shake my head. 'Even if you were old enough, you couldn't afford it. It's a lot of work, I gotta charge bank for it.'

'Could too. I got mad trade,' Cam says, his skinny chest puffing out a little.

'Yeah right, you do. You got some gangster scam running in the pre-teen dorm?'

Cam goes red.

'Well, tell me more about the stars then,' he says.

That I can do.

I tell him about Crux, the Southern Cross. Carina, visible all year round. Of Eridanus and Gemini in the summer, Lyra and Scorpius in the winter.

'And you know that big smeary, glowy thing in the sky that you can only see proper way out in the remotes? That's the Milky Way, that's the galaxy our planet's in,' I say, getting myself in deeper with everything I tell him, because then I've got to explain it all. 'It's shaped like a big spiral, like water spinning down the drain, yeah? And the way we see it is, kinda looking across it and out into the rest of space, so it looks like a band across the sky.'

I draw a big slash through the air with my soldering iron and he ducks a little, looking totally lost, but that's okay, he's nodding because he's getting the vibe of the story and I think he just likes hearing me tell it. For some weird reason I like telling it to him, too.

'And it's weird but back in the day, the Indigenous people saw the Milky Way as this big, like, Emu in the sky.'

'Emu like in the stew? That rubbery crap?' Cam asks.

'Yep. You ever been at the corps with the emu farms?'

He shakes his head.

'There's one out at Gilgandra. They're these huge birds . . .'

'Birds?' Cam's totally incredulous.

'Yeah, they're these giant birds but they don't fly. They've got long necks and long legs and they're the grumpiest fugging birds you ever saw, Cam. Like, worse than an Uncle on transpo duty.'

I can see Cam trying to picture a big angry bird like the way I've described it and I know it's jamming his brain circuits up and that he's for sure got it all wrong. I make a mental note to show him a picture on my tab one day.

'Anyway, they looked up at the Emu in the sky and depending on where it was and what shape it was in, cause it always changes, they could tell what time of the year it was and what they should be doing with their hunting and stuff. Like stealing emu eggs or whatever.'

'Why does it move?'

'Oh, because of, like the rotation of the earth and the orbit around the sun . . .'

I've lost him again. I bring him back with peeks of the thin blue-black dotted lines that link the little star shapes under my sleeves and my shirt and I try to describe where to look for Crux and the Emu in the big night sky.

'How'd you learn all this stuff?'

'Looked it up. When you sign up for the Free School you get a tab. Like, you gotta pay it off with extra duties and stuff, but it's yours and you can use it to look up anything you want. Well, anything that's not blocked by the corp, but you can find ways to get around it.'

'Yeah, a buncha kids in my dorms do school.'

'Well, if you signed up you could get a tablet and learn stuff too. Look up whatever you want. You could even get some extra training for when you age out.'

He twiddles the blue-handled pliers in his hands for a bit, pulling at the handles.

'It's too long. I won't age out for years.'

I snatch the tool from him before he ruins the rubber grips — they're the only good pair left.

'So what, you'll just fugg round 'til it's time to leave and then end up in a Prisoncorp when you can't get no work outside?'

'Probably.'

I clip him round the ear.

'Mahoney! Contact warning one!' bellows an Uncle walking up the row to our left. I throw my hands up and the Uncle makes a note. It's worth it.

'I used to think I'd never age out, but now I've got five days left. It goes so slow, Cam, until you look back and realise it went really fucking fast.' I jab the point of the pliers at him with every word and he ducks, shamed.

'Mahoney, language infraction!' the Uncle bellows. I twist my face up as he puts the strike against my name, but it's worth it.

'It's okay, kiddo,' I say. 'I don't hate you or nothing. I just don't want to see anyone stuck here forever.'

'Even Freya?'

'Not even Freya. Well . . . probably not.'

—

I scan the cafeteria 'til I find that unmistakable blonde head. Freya's on the other side, sitting alone. She's mashing her potatoes into a sad plateau on her plate, and even from all the way over here I can see the fierce look on her face.

'I've never known someone to get so mad at potatoes,' Vu says, stepping over the long plastic seat to slot in at the table beside me, her tray teetering in one hand.

'So, I don't want to hurt her or get in any trouble,' I say as Vu and I bump fists. 'I just want them to chuck her into the Time Out cells or maybe give her a fat old dose of kiddie Calmucet to space her out and keep her quiet 'til I leave.'

'She wouldn't tell on us,' Vu said around a mouthful of over-boiled broccoli.

'Wouldn't she? How do you know?'

'Well, she's got the whole loyalty thing going.'

Vu ponders for a bit. 'She's all "kids before skids", "damn the man", stuff like that.'

Cam slides in next to me with a tray and I unlock my tab screen and push it in front of him.

'That's an emu,' I whisper, pointing the picture I've pulled up.

'What the fug?' he says, and grabs it from me, studying the image intently. 'Are we having emu tonight?'

'Nah, I'm not sure what this is. Horse?' I take a big mouthful of the weird, grey meat and chew it thoroughly. 'Camel?' I chew a bit more and then throw my fork down. 'I have no idea. Whatever it is, it's terrible.'

'Welcome to Orphancorp,' Vu says. 'What did you expect? Cuts of the finest cow?'

'I'm a simple girl,' I say. 'I just like to be able to identify my food before I eat it.'

'Oooh, fancy.' Vu grins, her cheeks rounded with food and little green bits in all her teeth. What a babe.

I turn to Cam on my right and drop my voice.

'So Cam, what do you know about Freya? Do you think she's the type who'd spill? Like for revenge? If she, say, really hated some sweet and totally innocent babe who she thinks did her wrong?'

Cam thinks about it.

'I dunno. Maybe. Look what she did to your face.'

'Right? And let's say she's got some info on a certain piece of tech left in a certain Systower during what may or may not have been a mish last night . . .'

'That was you guys?' Cam hisses and I clap my hand over his mouth. He mumbles against my hand, more quietly this time, so I peel my palm away.

'You think she'd spill to Vile?'

'I don't know.' I feel the skin pull and pucker around the stitches on my cheek. 'That's why I'm asking you.'

'Shiz, Mirii. I couldn't say.'

'Maybe we could organise a cuddle party. Maybe some snugs might chill her out,' I say to Vu.

She shakes her head. 'She's never come to one.'

'Never? Wow.' I think on it for a bit. 'Maybe we should have one anyway. You know, just for the older kids.'

'You're gonna throw a cuddle party?' Cam asks.

'Yeah, maybe.'

'Can I come?' he asks.

'Ah . . . Um, I'm not sure you're going to be able to get out tonight. You know, after all the shiz last night,' Vu says.

'Maybe you could set one up for the pre-teen dorm,' I tell him.

He nods, like he's carefully considering something he hadn't thought of until now, then he grabs his tray and bolts off to a table full of pre-teen dormers and they all start whispering, excited-like.

I look at Vu and raise an eyebrow and she laughs, then I catch a glimpse of Freya behind us, spearing the last limp stalk of broccoli into her mouth.

Just before I turn away, she looks up and at me. My jaw clenches and my teeth press against each other, setting off the nerves in my rotten molars. I can just make out the black void in her smile where that missing tooth should go.

—

Ade gives us the all-clear, so I start. He's got an assignment for the Free School to finish and doesn't mind keeping lookout for us, though I promised him my next fruit from lunch anyway 'cause I don't like favours and Ade nods his thanks.

I'm cross-legged on the counter in the bathroom with Ara sat opposite, facing me.

'This is gonna hurt.'

'I know. I can handle it,' Ara says and with the look they give me, I can tell they're not lying. In those black-liquid eyes is a whole history of pain and I guess that this will be just another hurt on top of all the other hurts, but at least this pain will be real. With this kind of pain, the pain that you choose, at least you get to know when it ends. At least it *has* an end.

I glove up, unwrap a liner needle from a little sterile pack. When I first started out I jimmied up tools from whatever I could find around, but then, a while back, I gathered up the cash and got a sketchy Auntie to accept an e-parcel of some legit tools and ink. I feel, like, totally professional now, and virtually anti-septic.

I've drawn the name across the soft inside part of Ara's arm, just below the elbow ditch, in red pen. The letters sit inside a banner, with scrolled ends.

We begin and neither of us says a thing.

There's no sound but the drip of a tap into one of the metal sinks and the even whisper of our breath. I fall back into the steady rhythm of the needle like I never left, rocking into it, the shifting of the spike precise in my hands. The name takes shape gradually. My wrists start to ache.

When I get to halfway I pause and shake out my hand.

'Are you going to ask?' Ara says, their voice echoey in the empty bathroom.

'I figured you'd tell me if you wanted me to know,' I answer. I stretch my arms and roll my shoulders out. 'Ready to start again?'

Ara nods. 'I didn't think it would take this long.'

'How long did you think it would take?'

'I dunno. Not this long.' They prop their arm back on my leg and I get right to it, wiping the excess ink from the skin and dipping my needle into the little inkwell I've made out of aluminium foil.

'It's a lot of work,' I say. 'It used to take me longer.'

'How long have you been doing it? How did you learn?'

'Since I was about thirteen. A few kids in the house I was in did scummy pin-and-pencil tatts, and I thought they were so cool. I started looking stuff up and one day I saw a picture of this lady with blue lips and this pattern on her chin on the Wiki. I thought it was beautiful. Her tattoo is called a Moko and it's sacred to her people, the Maoris over in Kiwiland. It tells the story of their lives and their people and stuff. How rad is that? Anyway, yeah, I decided to learn and I practised on anyone who'd let me, which was pretty much everyone. There's a whole lotta kids out there with some shizzy-lookin' tattoos, thanks to me.'

'The tattoos tell the story of their lives?' Ara asks. I don't know if they heard anything else I said. They bite their lip as I move the needle to a new spot and start pressing it in, and in, and in.

'Yeah, in a roundabout kinda way. I mean, I don't do Moko 'cause I'm not a Maori but I feel like my tattoos kinda tell a bunch of stories about my life too.'

'Yeah. I get it. So you don't forget the important bits. Like a mark to make sure you remember.' Ara is nodding and looking sad and thoughtful.

'Yeah, I guess so.'

'The name. It's my sister. Our parents got caught up in the Queensland strife and we don't know what happened to them. She's a few years younger than me and when we came here I told her that I'd protect her, keep her safe. But they transferred her not long after we got processed in. I used hackies and bribed the admin to keep a track of where she was, but I lost her. She's not in the system any more.'

'Do you think she . . .' I don't even want to say it.

'No, she's not even listed as deceased, she's just gone. Like she wasn't ever in the system.'

I start on the last little piece, my wrist throbbing.

'I'm really sorry about your sister,' I say, making the last few jabs. I take a squirt of some antiseptic solution I stole from the first aid kit in my last dorm, and wipe away the excess ink.

The lines are dark and sharp against the soft skin of Ara's forearm, angry red fading to pink around the stark letters.

Raaya.

—

I lie in the dark, waiting for the time to come, the right time when you can feel the shift in the dorm from mostly awake to mostly asleep. I don't know how I can feel it, but it's plain to anyone. It's as if the room pulses with consciousness until it doesn't, 'til the thrum of caged kid-minds quiets to a low hum. When I feel it, I sit up. I can see a few other eyes scattered around, shining with excitement. I stand and gather my blankets and my pillow before I run down the little gap between the bunks, bare feet making a quiet thud, thud, thud on the linoleum.

Vu takes my arm when she gets close and we whisper between the beds. There's a bunch of us, a few of the oldest teens, snaking our way through the grey passages between each island of sleeping kids.

In the bathroom we all spread our covers out, throw our pillows around. Ara uses one of the blankets to block underneath the door. Everyone stands there for a second, sparks zapping between us all and eyes all gleamy then we all cuddle up on the floor, heads on bellies, feet in laps, arms draped across shoulders. Vu puts her head across my legs and I play with her hair, letting the soft strands slip over my palm, rubbing my fingertips over the buzzed parts. Blondie slides in next to me and puts his head on my shoulder, reaches up to take my free hand and I thread my fingers through his. He moves his hand over mine, calloused palm dancing across my palm. Ara comes over and puts Vu's feet in their lap and Vu starts to giggle softly as Ara's delicate fingers tickle her toes.

A little plastic bottle of potato punch appears from somewhere and we pass it around, taking sips. Blondie sparks a joint and some of us toke sips of that too.

My head's all swirly and it's like a weight lifts off the room, piece by piece, as everyone goes calm.

This is kinda sacred. It's our time.

In an Orphancorp, there's not a lot of physical contact, and the touches we do get usually hurt. Without each other, maybe we'd go through life thinking that hands are just slaps and fists, not for grasping or stroking.

The first cuddle party I remember, I must have been about four. A boy walked past me late in the night, caught a glimpse of my open eyes.

'Come on,' he said. 'It's time to hug now.'

I followed him, and a bunch of other kids were there, tangle-haired and sleep-sweaty in their giant nightshirts. We pushed a bunch of pillows together and everyone flopped onto them, pressing up against each other. We lay like that a long time. There were quiet sobs now and again. Some of the kids fell asleep. I clung tight to a little girl about my age and her red hair got all in my mouth. Then, the little limbs began to move and everyone just kinda came awake again and we unthreaded ourselves from each other, pulled the pillows apart, and went back to our beds.

I lay there, alone, but the warmth from the others still on my skin and a different kind of warmth inside me, something I hadn't felt before, or for a long time. Like I was part of something. Like I was loved, even just for thirty minutes in the middle of the night.

I'm feeling pretty loved right now, a dozy web of limbs woven around me and Vu is at my neck, nuzzling into it and Blondie is on the other side, nibbling on my earlobe and there's always this tipping point, this critical mass moment when all the chemicals in the room shift and turn electric. Sometimes it doesn't happen, and we all just snug and sleep like at cuddle party when we were kids, but more often than not, we reach that point and then? It's on. Sometimes it's just-touchies or everything-but-pants. Sometimes, like now, it's anything-goes.

Vu's mouth is on mine and Ara is at her belly, lifting up her nightie and burying their face in her side which makes her sigh under my lips. Blondie's hands are on my waist as he kisses up my neck. Then, somehow, Vu is devouring Blondie and I'm lying close by Ara, our tongues twining gently and I feel their hands all over me and I go to lift their nightshirt but Ara bats my hands away.

'No,' Ara says. 'I'm not . . . I can't . . .'

'It's okay,' I whisper. I drop the fabric and wrap my arms around their neck instead. I let the delicate hands explore me as I run my fingers down through skeins of soft dark hair. Vu crawls back over and I peel off her nightie as Blondie slips in beside Ara and I watch them kiss as Vu undresses me too.

The room is alive with harsh breaths and sighs, everyone's in convoluted little groups that split off and merge with others. Someone's got a stash of black market condoms and everyone's digging in and giggling and the air is full of the sounds of quiet sighs, laughter and foil packets ripping open.

I close my eyes and let the zinging in the air carry

me off. There's bodies moving around me, sweet lips on my belly, sweet lips pressed on my mouth. In the dark behind my eyelids, I am all embodied, like out of my head and not just because I'm drunk and stoned but because I'm not stuck in the swirl of my thoughts, I'm all arms and legs and torso and neck and fingers and the pulsing little core between my legs and then I hear a whisper.

'Open your eyes, Mirii.'

It's Vu. The dark splits and lets in the moonlight, glinting off limbs and eyes-closed, mouth-open faces and she's there. I look right into her and she into me and then everything turns to sparks. When I can breathe again, we kiss.

I feel so connected to everyone, and we all lie in a big, sweaty pile for as long as we can, trying to keep the threads between us whole. I feel like something inside me is full, and the easy swirl of thoughts that come from a mind free of fear. I didn't realise how scared I was until I stopped feeling scared for a minute. Scared to leave, scared something might happen and I might have to stay, scared of the void in Freya's smile and the empty-bed cold in Warden Kyle's eyes.

'You done?'

Everyone lifts their heads at once. Freya's standing in the doorway, framed by the door and the dark room behind it.

I hold out my arms. 'Come cuddle with us, Freya. Let's be friends.'

'You're all disgusting.' She walks past us to the toilet and sits. Her pee spatters against the porcelain and into the water, loud like a waterfall. The explosive sound of the flush shreds the webs between us all and suddenly it's not a magic warm pile of loving bodies, it's a sweat-drying, cold-creeping bunch of stupid kids on the floor of a dark bathroom in the middle of the night.

'Way to harsh our refractory period, Freya,' I say.

'Do you think you're smart or something, with your big words?' she says.

'Well, yeah,' I tell her. Everyone's getting up and getting dressed and grumbling and this is not how cuddle party should end.

'Why you gotta come in and bugger up our good time?' Blondie says, sliding his pants up and hunting around for a shirt until he remembers he wasn't wearing one and then just stands there, arms crossed over his sweaty abs, glowering.

'You don't mess with cuddle party, Freya. This is, like, the only time we have that isn't totally shitty,' says Ara, smoothing hair down around their stormy face.

'What? I just took a whizz. You're acting like I'm the foot basher on duty in the Naughty Chair, for fuck's sake.'

'You wouldn't understand,' Vu says, gathering up her pillow and her blanket. 'It's special.'

'It's gross. I bet you all have the megaclap or something, flopping around together like that.' She goes out through the door and everyone looks at each other and the spell's been most definitely broken, so we just head, one by one, back to bed.

FOUR DAYS

Vu trails behind as I drag my feet to my mattress. I only know she's there when she reaches out for me.

'Mirii,' she says, not whispering, just speaking really low. Whispers hiss and echo across the big room, but soft voices get lost between the walls and rows and sleep sounds.

She and I sit, perching on the edge of my bunk, the vinyl cover groaning with our weight and a few of the lumps around us shifting and mumbling in their sleep at the sound.

'Way to ruin cuddle party,' she says, awkward, as if we didn't just have this convo back in the bathroom. It's weird and sad to see her like this, but I feel the same way. It's just weird and sad all around.

I've got lots of things to say about it, but all I can manage is, 'Yeah.'

'Yeah . . .' she says and we stare at the floor for a minute, almost touching. It's funny to think that not thirty minutes ago, parts of me were in parts of her, parts of her were in parts of me. It's sad how that connection can get all busted up so easy.

'I like you, Mirii,' she spits out, suddenly. 'Like, like-like.'

'I like, like-like you too, Vu.'

'But I don't want to. Not 'cause you're shiz or anything, but you're gonna leave soon.'

'Yeah,' I say. 'Me too.'

See, this is why I don't like-like anyone. Or that other one, the one we don't ever say. Because, eventually, everyone gets taken away.

'Yeah,' she sighs and we hold hands for a bit.

The silence hurts, sorta twists inside my chest.

'You could come find me,' I say. 'How long 'til you age out?'

'Seven months,' she says. 'If I don't muck it up.'

'We should try. You ever seen the old Town Hall building, right in the middle of Sydney?'

'No,' she says. I haven't seen it either, but I've seen pictures and I know people have organised to meet up there because it's so easy to find.

'It's one of the only old buildings left there. It's real small, and it's kinda like this tiny stone place in the middle of all these huge scrapers, yeah? You can look it up. We could meet there. There's a set of steps out front. Let's say, in seven months and one week, we meet on the steps at 6 p.m.?'

She brightens a bit. I do too.

'Yeah? You reckon?'

'Heaps reckon. If we still got the like-like, then we can do whatever we want, you know? If not, we can still be friends, hang out on the outside. See what that's like.'

'That's rad,' she says and she leans into me. We sit there, like that, for a bit. Then I lift her chin up and we're kissing again and she climbs up on me and I grip her waist, her hips, her bum, through her night-shirt and we do that for a bit, too.

—

'So, did you have your little pre-teen snugger session last night?' I ask Cam, elbowing him as I reach over for a mag-tip mini-driver.

He flushes so pink that I swear the tips of his ears are like, fire extinguisher red.

'I'll take that as a yes,' I say, elbowing him a few more times for fun.

'Did you guys not want me to come to your cuddle party because . . .'

'Because it's different from yours?'

'Yeah.'

'Well, yeah, but I wasn't gonna say that. Are things starting to get a bit weird at the pre-teen cuddle party?'

He doesn't say anything, just goes even redder,

though I thought that wasn't possible. He's almost purple.

I'm struggling to get this tab back together, I don't wanna be too forceful, but being so gentle is getting me nowhere. We're done with our consignment of headphones and everyone else is wiring lamps together now, but me and a few others are on special duty, fixing up a load of junked tabs for all the kids in the freeschool program. I'm gleeful as anything because I've got mad skills with this sort of thing, and Cam's super keen to learn from the best.

He's not keen to look right at me right now, though. I peer up at him with teasy-eyes.

'So Cam, did you get some touchy-feely last night? Feel up any new boobs? Noobs?'

'Shut up!' he says, but he knows I'm just ripping on him. You always gotta rip on the ones you like the best.

'You gotta be gentle with those noobies, Cam. They're *sore* when they're just coming out like that . . .'

He pushes on my shoulder, still red and all sheepish and I can tell by the way he's looking at me, or not looking at me, that he probably did. Good for him.

'It happens like that once you get to your age,' I say. 'One cuddle party we were all just snugging each other and doing comfort stuff, and the next it was as if something in the air changed. Like the way we smelled just drove us crazy and we all went to a new place. It's fun though.'

Cam nods, all thoughtful and I feel kinda good that I'm here to say this to him. I had to figure all this junk out on my own. 'Just relax and go with it. Try and be safe, there's always condoms around if you know where to look for 'em. Don't do anything you don't want to do and don't make anyone feel like they have to do anything. If someone says something's cool and another thing's not, you gotta respect that, 'cause everyone is different, you know?'

'Did you and Vu . . .? At your cuddle party?'

It's my turn to go a little red.

'Yeah, yeah we did some stuff,' I say and it's not like me to be coy or anything, but here I am, being coy.

'You like her. I can tell. She likes you too,' Cam says.

'I don't know. I'm . . . not good with this kind of thing. And I'm leaving so soon, so what's the point?'

We both go quiet for a bit and let the clip and crump of the buzzshop take over for a while, my fingers fiddling with the inner-works of a battered Orion tab.

'Are you scared?' Cam asks out of nowhere.

For a second, all the things I'm scared of start tumbling through my head like a tonne-load of socks and undies in the giant tumble-dryer down in the laundry.

'Shizless,' I say. Then, 'of what?'

'Of leaving.'

'Oh, yeah. Totally,' I tell him, holding out a hand and flicking my fingers twice before he passes me a tiny screw from the square I'd drawn on a sheet of old paper. It's a diagram of the tab I've just pulled apart, with labels and squares for all the parts. *So you don't lose nothing*, he'd said. *That's genius.*

'You got a job out there?' Cam asks, placing the next screw in my hand before I need to wave at him.

'Nah, no job.'

'What about a place to live?' he asks as I fit the screw to the head of the mag-driver and twist it home.

'No. Not yet.'

'Wow. How come? When Byron Kirk left, he had work *and* a bed at a boarding place.'

'Well, isn't Byron Kirk a shining fugging example of life post-Orphancorp?'

'Shiz, Mirii, I'm just asking.'

I feel all jammed up on the inside, scared and my brain can't cope with it, so I'm just voiding it with anger. It's not even Cam's fault, he's just here, just pointing out things that are true. I hand him the tab and he cleans the screen with a rag dipped in Mrs Sparkle Screen Cleaner, then slips it into a softcover in a box at our feet. He brings up a fresh tab and I get to opening her up.

'I don't know why I haven't sorted anything out yet. I just . . . can't. It's like every time I try I can't make it past opening the browser on my tab. It just don't feel real yet.'

'Oh. That makes sense, I guess,' Cam says.

I don't have to explain anything else because the buzzer starts to drone for lunch. I'd take a half-cooked brumby stew over this line of questioning any day.

—

The hall is crowded with kids coming in from the workshops but I still spot Vu coming out of the dorms, her long hair gathered into a half-falling-out twisty bun on one side, the fine buzz of the shaved part showing her pale scalp through.

'Hey Vu,' Cam calls and she turns. Her eyes are almost swollen shut and there's tears all on her face and it takes me a second to realise what's going on. When I spot her backpack, stuffed full and gripped tight to her chest, extra boots swinging from one of the arms, clarity kinda rushes in.

She's being transferred.

Cam hasn't seen it yet, probably because he's too short to see over the line of kids shuffling in for lunch, so he's confused when I start running after her. There's three other kids with her, all bag-clutching and looking scared. There's got to be some mistake. The Aunties and Uncles always serve the transfer notice three full days beforehand, so how did she not know? Why would she tell me she like-liked me if she knew she was gonna leave?

'Vu!' I say and she turns, almost tripping on the bru

in front of her and she drops her backpack. I grab it from the floor for her.

'What's happening?' I ask, pressing the thick canvas bag into her chest.

'I'm being transferred!'

'Where? How? Did you get notice?' I say, as she pulls me along in the line with her. Aunt Bev is at the head, leading them down the hall, but she hasn't seen me yet.

'No! I don't know what's happening. They pulled me outta the nursery half an hour ago and told me to pack my things.'

'There has to be a mistake,' I say and I jog up ahead. Aunt Bev scowls at me.

'Outta the way, Maroney.'

'It's Mahoney, Aunt Bev. So, where you taking this lot off to?' I try to sound light and breezy like I'm just curious but I'm puffing hard and my face is all creased and she can totally tell that I don't just have a general line of inquiry going on here.

'None of ya business. Now, mind yourself and get to lunch before I give you a mark.' She heads off through the door of the admin area and it's out of bounds so I just stop on instinct but Bev keeps going and the transfer kids all follow her. Vu pauses on the threshold and she's crying hard and I feel a few hot tears spill down my face when she wraps her arms around me. I grip her tight.

'You two!' Bev shouts from the door. 'Contact warning one!'

We ignore her.

'Don't forget me,' she says.

'I won't. You remember me too.' I squeeze her tighter.

'Contact warning two! Vu, get your arse through that door. I will not tell you twice,' Bev thunders at us.

'I'll find you. I'll get a hackie to track you for me.'

She nods, pressing snot and tears into my neck. I pull back and lift her face, kiss her lips, tasting the salt she's made all over the place.

'Contact warning three!' Bev says, and suddenly there's rough hands pulling us apart. They turn her around and she's through the door, getting smaller and further away.

'Mahoney! Admin area is out of bounds!' bellows some faceless Uncle behind me and I ignore him and race across the threshold.

'Vu! Seven months and one week! Town Hall steps. Come find me!' I call and they're pulling her so she can't look back but I know she's heard. I stop and my shoulders kind of sag because she's out the door now. She's gone. I should have known. I shouldn't have let the like-like creep in.

Then the impact comes.

I've seen folks tackled by a bunch of Uncles all at once, but managed to avoid it so far. It's not like

I don't get up to naughty things, it's just that I don't often get caught. But it's pretty easy to get caught when you're standing in the middle of the admin wing, a good five metres across the yellow-dash line on the floor that indicates out-of-bounds. I'm in their den now, a different world of buzzing systowers and keyboard clicks, of bad kid-jokes and the rustle of junk-bar wrappers. I'm out of place and standing there like a giant whitehead on the tip of a nose, just waiting to get squeezed.

And squeezed I get.

The impact is what I imagine it might be like to get hit by a bus. One minute, my boots are flat-footed on the lino, the next, they're in the air and so am I, three thick, sweaty Uncles sweeping me up with their trajectory and we all hit the floor. My body breaks their fall and the sound of it feels like the pain. All the breath presses out of my chest and I can't suck in another. They climb off me and one flips me over and twists my arm back behind me, jams a knee into my spine that might hurt if I wasn't already in pain.

Then he lets me go.

I know why.

'I'm down,' I say, even though it doesn't matter. 'I'm down already.'

When the kiddie-prod hits and the first jolt zings through, I think I can hear them laughing. Then I can't hear much at all.

—

I'm not out for long, because I come back when they're dragging me into the hallway and I can't imagine they would have left me cluttering up the floor in admin for too long.

'That's a strike, Mahoney. We're feeling generous today. You're lucky you aren't hangin' upside-down in the Consequence wing right now.' The Auntie drops my legs and steps over me, back into admin.

'Mirii! Mirii, you okay?' Cam is there. Ara and Blondie too, and a whole lot of kids all come 'round me and I'm blinking hard and gasping like an asthmatic before a puff.

'Did . . . Did I . . . Did I . . .'

'What, Mirii, what are ya trying to say?' Cam asks, taking my hand while Ara squeezes the other.

'Did I whizz myself this time?'

The kids all around giggle and the tension starts to slip away.

'No, not this time,' Blondie says. He brushes everyone away, the little kids scattering back into the cafeteria and he gets his hands underneath me and scoops me up. He carries me back into the dorm and sends Cam down to get me some food and water from the lunchline. He puts me down, real gentle, onto my bed. Ara and a few other kids from cuddle party last night hover around and there's a crowd around the door that hums and jostles, looking in to make sure I'm okay.

'What happened?' Ara says.

'It's Vu, she got transferred,' I tell them, my teeth still chattering.

'Transfers don't happen on Sundays,' says Ara, hand jammed to their mouth, nerve-biting the long nails tipping each delicate finger.

'It's Sunday?' I ask.

I always forget it's Sunday. The days all bleed together because it's all just get up, work, sleep. But on Sundays, we get three hours out in the playground in the afternoon. Playtime.

'Oi, you little jerks. Go outside and play,' booms a thin-haired blonde Auntie, scattering the crowd at the door. 'Get some bloody sunshine,' she says, popping her head in through the doorway and glowering at us. 'Now!'

Everyone helps me up and Blondie and Ara hold my arms while I jerk and shuffle out along the hall, my heart still racing and the blood pumping in my ears, making a hollow noise that sounds like, *Vu, Vu, Vu.* We go past the workshops, past the stairs to the Consequence wing and out the door to the playground. I'm not sure that I'd consider it playful exactly: a blank asphalt square, weeds coming up through the cracks, fence-lined and barb-wire topped. But the air is fresh out here and the sun feels warm on my face.

They set me up at a splintered wooden table and Cam comes flying out the door and hurtling across the yard. He passes me a mandarin secreted in his armpit.

'Present,' he says. 'From the kids on Foodservice. They told me to give you this too.'

He touches me, gentle like a pillow or a kiss, on my arm. Comis. 'Cause a tasing hurts, so here's a thing that doesn't. I still feel my muscles vibrate under his hand, but it helps.

'I guess it's from me too,' he says. 'I'm sorry about Vu.'

I can't even force a smile because of all the hurt bubbling up just under my skin. I don't want to cry. I'm not going to cry, I can't, not here where everyone can see, but my eyes feel all gleamy with tears and everything blurs. I can feel my throat forcing up the sobs. *Not here, not here.*

'Thanks little bru,' I say, hardly able to get it out. I want to hug him, but Cam is already going all red so I punch him in the guts instead and he groans and shakes his head, going, 'nah, nah.' He tears off to join a bunch of kids playing some kind of weird balance game that I bet only they know the rules to.

One by one, or in little groups, kids come up to me, their faces flush with the air and the excitement, or the twin games of full-contact netball and bullrush going on in each corner of the yard. Some nod, some offer a solemn fist for bumping, most just place a hand on my arm or my shoulder.

Tangles, the storyteller from the kiddie dorm yesterday, she must remember me because she runs up and leaps onto my back, holding me tight for a good thirty seconds before an Auntie from her dorm watch screams at her from across the yard.

'Tompkins! Contact warning!'

Tangles drags herself up off me.

'Sorry you got tased, ghost-lady,' she says, and skips away. Little weirdo.

I'm touched for the comis, because these kiddos barely know me and they're making my heart hurt like whoa crazy, even more than before. It's the kinda hurt that aches from all sides.

—

Outside the bathroom I can hear kids banging and bitching as they go about their mandatory Sunday afternoon chores but here in my tile and porcelain enclave there's just me and the quiet hum of a busted toilet filling and leaking, filling and leaking.

My hand is still shaking but I'm making the shape anyway. The little trembles in the line will make me remember. I press and press, the points of the needle driving a hot pain through me, my neck aching from the angle, my wrist twisted and fingers pressure-white from how tight I'm gripping. I want to get the ink deep in there. I want to make the line as black and true as the night.

And it's not just for Vu and how I like-like her or whatever, this one's for everything. The way they can just take someone away one day and not even tell anyone why. The way they can keep those poor busted mish kids down in Consequences and do what they do to them, and no one knows and if they did, I doubt anyone would care. How they've had me working since I was six years old, how they teach us to read and write but make us pay to learn anything else, the way they lock us in together at night and let kids do what they're gonna do to make more babies for them.

How it's a cycle. How we're set up to fail.

When I'm done I keep my shirt hiked up and stare at the tattoo in the mirror, the black shape like a beacon branded into the soft brown skin above my belly, below my breasts.

V. For Vu, of course. For Vile. For voltage and vomit. For Verity House. For vengeance?

Yeah, maybe for vengeance, too.

—

'Who is this dipshiz?' I whisper, trying not to let him hear me.

'Berry. Costa Berry,' says Ara.

We're all jammed up by the door. Blondie's the tallest, so he's peeking through the window, taking quick little sips of the view and updating us on the stats.

'Well, what's he good for?' I say, my voice real low, but he still looks over at me.

'He's a hackie,' Ara tells me.

'He's like, twelve?' I hiss and he looks over at me.

His curly brown hair is just a bit too long and it spills down over his oil-slick forehead. He's a whole head and a half shorter than I am, with shifty eyes and every few seconds he clears his throat, this thin, weedy 'ahem' that drives me crazy. Every time he does it, I dare him to do it just one more time.

Wouldn't you know it, there he goes again.

'I'm, ahem, I'm almost fourteen,' he says, hitching up his pyjama pants. They're so long they bunch and puddle around his feet, and this just adds to the little-doofus vibe I get from him.

'He's really good,' Ara says, and I guess I trust them.

Just then Blondie waves for us all to get back. A torchlight shines in through the window and I can see the glass steam up where the Uncle presses his nose as he peers through. They're supposed to come in and shine the light around, but they never do. Who could be bothered? I mean, the door's locked, right?

The yellow beam slices right between us, me and Blondie on one side of the doorway, Ara and the little pinhead on the other. What was his name? Barry? Betty? Berry, that's it. We all crouch there, totally still and the light disappears finally. Footsteps echo away and Berry clears his throat again.

'You better get your airways under control before we go out there,' I tell him, but Blondie's up at the window again and he flaps his hand for us to be quiet.

'Uncle Rick's off to the dunnies. He usually takes at least ten minutes. Time to slam this shit,' he says and slips the key into the lock, quiet and careful as anything. The door cracks just a hair and we peek out.

The hall is empty but for the buzz of the lights dotted up and down the hall. I think of the grey ghosts for a second, their lonely games of hidey-findey in the halls and all my hairs stand on end. Behind me, Blondie wraps his head in a spare shirt. He's wearing two, one on his face, one on his back, which is twice as many shirts as I've ever seen him in.

He slips out the door first and works his way up the hall, inching along the wall. When he gets to the corner, he monkeys up the wall like it's nothing, springing off doorknobs and finding purchase in the cracks in the wall. To be fair, some of those cracks are pretty wide so it's only like, impressive rather than magic or anything. Blondie hangs lightly off the bracket for the cam, shoulder jammed into the corner and bare toes crammed into a decent gap. He slings a pillowcase over the cam, long end dangling for easy grabbing on our way out. After the last mishbust, we're not taking chances with the cameras - they might actually be working now.

The moment it's covered, we all flood out the door,

closing it gently behind us. Ara's long hair trails as they tiptoe to the end of the hall, by the back door and the stairs to the Consequence wing, on lookout. Blondie jumps down, landing lightly on his feet and stays beneath the bracket for a quick jump-rip of the camera cover if we've gotta make a hasty exit. I push Berry out in front of me and we go right to the sys-tower behind the watch desk. He slams a flash bead in the back and picks up one of the watch tabs.

'See, passwords for the main OS with all our records changes every day at midnight and, ahem, I've made this patch that temporarily changes the time to midnight and then changes it to MY password, so . . .' Berry says softly, his fingers dull-thudding over the keyscreen on the tab.

'Shhhh,' I say. 'I don't need to know how it works, just get me on there.'

We wait an agonising sixty seconds for the fake-clock to click over and before I even know it, he's on the OS, navving through to the state ward records.

'Vu . . . Vu . . . Hey, was she that Vietnamese girl with the shaved bit in her hair and, ahem, ah, the thick glasses?'

'Yes, that's her,' I tell him. 'Please be quiet.'

'Ahem, sorry. I liked her.'

'We all like her, that's why we want to find her.'

'Um . . . She's not in here,' Berry says, peering up at me, his face bottom-lit by the glowing tab screen.

'She's not even in here at all. Are you sure that's how you spell her name?'

I grab the tab off him and hiss, 'Of course I'm sure, it's two fugging letters!'

I scroll through. Vreen, Kevin. Vu, Aiden. She should be right in between them. I page through every Vu on the screen. No Adeline. No record, no transfer, not even an awful, red-tinged deceased page.

Just nothing.

Ara races down the hall, their footsteps quick and quiet.

'I heard a flush!' they whisper, and Berry leans over the desk, pulls his flash bead patch out of the systower and races back into the dorm room before I even realise what's happening.

'Hurry,' Blondie says and I wave him off.

'Just go, I need one more second.'

He leaps up to grab the shirt over the camera, blonde hair flying. I turn away from the camera and I scroll through 'V' again, eyes skittering over the text.

Uncle Rick doesn't come whistling around the corner, like I expect him to at any second. I hear another flush and I grimace at the thought of what he's doing in there. It's a false alarm, he's not on his way at all.

So it's not his hand that clamps over my shoulder, cold and hard and tight-pinching the nerves there. It's not his voice that startles me into dropping the tethered watchdesk tab on the floor, the screen cracking into a thousand little fissures, each one capturing the moonlight and the darkness of the hall in turn. It's not his words that come, stinging my ear like acid, chilling my spine like an icy shower in the Consequence wing, which is where I'm off to, by the way. No doubt about it.

'Out of bed? Mahoney, is it?'

It's Vile. It's Warden Kyle.

And of course I can't help it. Me and my mouth. Like maybe he's gonna go easy on me if I just cower and grovel, but I figure if I'm already up the scheisse creek, how's a paddle gonna help me anyway?

'Yeah,' I say, turning to give him a grin and I bend down and peck him on the cheek. 'I thought I'd come and give ya a goodnight kiss, Vile.'

THREE DAYS

It doesn't feel real until after Vile's had the Uncles and Aunties on nightshift run a sweep of the halls, wakes all the kids up in the teen dorm, questions them in front of me, questions me in front of them. After he smashes the already shattered watch tablet to pieces, makes all the kids in the room jump. After he tears my mattress to bits, but doesn't find anything, even though I swear I put my tab back in my hidey-hole. After he drags me out of the room by the hair and I get a good long look at Ara and Blondie with their angryscared eyes, at Freya, who's got this weird combination of glee and pity on her mug. After Vile marches me down the hall.

—

After I realise what's coming to me, but before I get it.

—

I'm not getting out of here. I'm not going to try and make a life for myself. I'm going right to Consequences, to face 'em, then into Time Out for as long as they like. The broken tablet is 'destruction of property' and I try to remember what the Consequences of that are, try do the maths in my head to see if that's enough to send me over to a Prisoncorp, but the maths are arbitrary anyway, and besides, Vile's got me so tight around the arm that I can feel his fingers slip into the spaces between my muscles and tendons and I can't keep a track of much else.

The hallway is endless and far too short at the very same time. There's a growing group around me, led by Uncle Rick who's looking vicious because this happened on his watch and he'll cop a strike or a salary dock. By the flash in his eyes I can see that he's going to make me pay for it, in bruises and in blood.

The watch must be down to a skeleton crew because half the nightshifters come down to herd me towards the stairs. They laugh and joke and their eyes sparkle and some of their faces are flush red with excitement, which makes my guts twist and all the feeling drain out of my fingers and feet.

I don't bother saying anything. It's not gonna help and anyway, my mouth's gone so dry that I don't think I could squeak out a word.

The door to the stairwell looms up in my vision and I close my eyes as Vile kicks it open and pushes me through. The crash of the door against the wall bounces off the cinderblock walls and all around my head.

Down we go.

—

'Children need to know the Consequences of their actions.'

Vile tells me this over and over.

I'm not sure if it's blood or sweat or water that's dripping down my face. All those things? I'm sure my stitches have busted open and it is hot down here, plus my hair's still wet from the tub of water that's now red-tinged and forgotten by the door. The room feels airless. And electric, but not in the good way. It zaps with the kind of charge that grows in the space between the ones with the power and the ones without.

'Who helped you?' someone says. 'Who else?' they ask and they pull the balled up rag out of my mouth to let me splutter the same answer, which is not the answer they want.

'Just me,' I say. 'Just me.'

Back in it goes.

The chair isn't really a chair, it's more a swivelling kind of platform. I think the base of it was once a chair, but the top is a plank of wood. My knees ache against it. My hands are behind my back, but tethered to a spot on the ceiling, pulled up. I've been here for hours, maybe days. Maybe I've always been here. Every muscle in me screams, screams. Every part of me is ripe here, unable to be hidden. The soles of my feet take precedence now. An Auntie, her face flushed and dripping sweat, holds my face up to hers.

'Look at me,' she says.

I look to her left, to the pokey. A pair of frightened eyes peers from the cutout and I lock onto them.

'Look at me,' she says again, pulling my hair, my head, back. I remember pulling Vu's head back like this, but that was with lust, for pleasure. This is different. It's funny how the intention changes the action. I try to focus and lock my stare with the eyes in the pokey, try to make out who it is. The person behind those eyes aches for me, and for themselves. I ache for the pokey. The press of all the pointed bits driven through the steel locker walls seems gentle in comparison, peaceful. I could be alone.

'Don't look at him,' the Auntie says. She lets go of my head and picks up the hose, turns the tap until water jets out. She takes it to the pokey, shoves it though the cutout and closes the slider, trapping it there. There are gurgles and screams. Water glugs out through holes in the bottom and down the drain in the middle of the room.

'Look at me,' she says, and I have to pick my own

head up this time. The chair wobbles and I almost tip off the side. My shoulders beg me not to tip. They don't want to twist that way in their sockets, but they will, if they have to. They'll jump right out. I've seen it. It doesn't look real when it happens but I bet it feels real and I don't want to find out.

I look at her and she pulls the rag out of my mouth.

'Who else?'

'Just me,' I say. This is not the answer she needs.

'Children need to learn the Consequences of their actions,' Vile says from off in the corner, far enough away to stay clean, close enough to see. Everyone laughs. I laugh. It's funny, or it's not, or I just don't know what else to do.

When the impacts come again, I try to keep myself upright. The pains just all slip into one, like a crescendo of noise or tone or a buzzing in my ear, but in all the parts of me instead. I look around, through the shifting bodies of the Aunties and Uncles, their twisted faces. It's bright in here. Brighter than anywhere else, and never dark. The cinderblock is white, or white-ish. The tiled floor is white, or white-ish. There's a red ring around the drain below. There's a bank of lights above, uncaring white light. Two steel lockers to my left, dotted with screw and nail-heads, sharp ends pointing inwards. Down the hall to the right, the Time Out cells. The concrete walls ring with breaths, hard like gunshots, dull thuds of things striking flesh, the pulse of the hose, the gurgling drain, the buzz of the fluorescence.

I wonder if the grey ones are watching me from up there while they feast on that buzz.

—

They say you leave little bits of yourself behind in the Time Out cells. It's another kind of ghost story the kids tell each other in blanket-gatherings late at night. They say that every day you spend here grates another piece off you that seeps into the walls.

I believe it. Time Out feels haunted, but not like the hallways upstairs at night with their grey ghosts. These thick walls are full of fragments, little bits of everyone that's lost themselves in here. The time here diminishes a kid, takes away pieces they can't ever get back.

I wonder what parts I'll leave here? Hopefully it's something I won't need.

'I'll leave you the big mole with the hair coming out of it on my bum, yeah?'

My voice bounces around the concrete walls. It sounds thick and fuzzy coming out of my torn-up lips. I run my tongue around my mouth and I'm relieved to find all my teeth still there, though a couple of them have split through the fragile skin of my lips.

I try to stand, but can't. There's nothing in here to

pull myself up on. There's almost nothing in here at all. Just a bucket for my waste. And me. I'm in here too. That's a bit of a waste as well. Or maybe I'm waste. I'm not sure.

Everything else is concrete. It's cold. I shrug off my nightshirt and bunch it up underneath me, but then my naked back presses against the wall and the chill creeps inside me, my bones going cold. It's so hot upstairs, the heat rising all day, so how is it so cold down here? Is it because we're underground? Is it because of the ghost-bits in the walls?

The cell's about the size of a toilet cubicle, but with no toilet, and a high ceiling. The paint on the cracking walls is white, or was. Grime and piss and dirt and blood stain everything, gather in the creases, between the concrete blocks, in the corners. It's tall enough to stand in, and sit, and lie down if you curl up, but not to stretch out.

Give it enough time and it will be my whole world. I've been here before. Not here, but here enough. Time Out cells are all the same. Time gets lost here, along with other things. When the cutout slides open and the food comes through I try to make a note of it, try to remember to count them, but I know I won't be able to. The bread is stale and the water warm. I shuffle so I'm close to the door, peering through the crack, hair-wide, and watch the shadow of shoes passing.

I roll onto my back and I cry.

I wonder where I'll go now. To a Prisoncorp? Wherever they sent Vu? Will I die in here? I've seen it happen. When I was buying out my second tab after the first stopped working, they put me on cleanup in Time Out on the weekends. I saw two blue bodies secreted up the stairs. Will that be me? Do I have blood rushing into my guts right now that will send me out slowly, writhing on the floor? Is that how I'll get out of here?

I never let myself really think about getting out. Like for-real out, into the world.

At first you don't because it's so long away. And then you don't because it's just so close.

Like, most kids will be diligent and get a dorm set up in the city, send in apps for jobs even though landing a job is like spotting a maggot in a pot of rice. Sure, it can happen but it's a slog.

I never did that. I don't know why. Maybe some bit of me knew it would end like this. I thought I had this well of hope or whatever inside me, but maybe I didn't.

Or maybe I do, and that's the bit I'll leave behind here.

TWO DAYS

The lights don't go off. They don't ever go off. They hum and zzz all day, all night, so you can't tell the difference and time gets all muddled.

Because there's nothing to look at, my mind fills in the blanks, the blank walls. First it's little twisting shapes in the corners of my eyes that I try to catch but always miss. After a while, forests of patterns grow in each cinderblock screen. I'm having whole conversations in my head, doing things differently with different outcomes, trying for different Consequences. They all lead me in here, to this room and I am convinced it is inevitable.

It was always going to end like this.

When Vu appears in the corner, whole and full-bodied, even I know that it's going too far, that I took one-too-many knocks to the head region. Vu is gone, she's been taken somewhere secret and scrubbed off the sys, or worse, she's filling out a shallow grave somewhere, but she's not here.

Still, I wonder for a second if ghost-Vu would be warm if I tried to hold her.

—

The food comes through the cutout. It could be anything; breakfast, lunch or dinner. It's not just bread and water this time, there's a little bowl of grey-meat and a mandarin. Someone upstairs paid a hefty price for this treat for me and the smell of the meat makes hot saliva squirt out from under my tongue and fill up my mouth. I shovel it in right there at the little shelf under the cutout, a pair of dark, dark eyes set in brown skin peering through the slit and watching me with sorrow and pity.

The mandarin. It reminds me of Vu, that first night that she shared the fruit with me. When I break open the skin the little cell fills up with the sweet citrus smell.

Underneath it is a little slip of paper.

Psynode, it says.

Brainfuckers, Inc.

Vu? it says. Then, *Vile knows.*

I crumple the paper. I eat it. I can feel the ink seeping off the paper and into my blood. I'll remember what it says forever.

ONE DAY

When Aunt Bev comes through the door I get a shock because it's like I forgot what the door was there for.

'Get up, Mahoney,' she says, and when I try and fall back onto the concrete floor, she holds a hand out for me.

I stare at it for a bit. It's as strange as if she was holding out a flower towards me, or a loaded rifle.

'Get up, Mahoney, now. There's not a lot of time.' Aunt Bev reaches down and takes my hand in hers, pulling me to my feet, my feet that sing and ache and cramp as I step out of the door of my Time Out cell.

'How long have I been here?' I ask her, my voice defeated and stew-thick and garbled around my swollen lips. 'Which Prisoncorp are you gonna take me to?'

'Bloody hell, Mirii, dramatic much? You've been in here a day and a half.'

Oh.

'And you aren't going to any Prisoncorp,' she says.

'You've got Age Transfer. I'm taking you upstairs to admin for processing.'

I can hear the words she says, but I don't know why she's saying them or how or what they mean. Is this real?

'But . . . Vile, I mean, Kyle, said . . .'

She stops in the middle of the Consequences hallway. I can see the room with the chair and the pokies just off to the left. It's clean now, the floor dry like nothing happened. But when I look at the cutout I see the flash of a pair of eyes and I feel like I can't breathe so I look away.

'The Warden says a lot of things. I follow the system,' Bev says and she holds up her tab. The words on the bright white screen swim in my vision. 'OS says you Age Transfer today, so I'm getting you ready for release, Mahoney. Now, let's get a move on.'

'But . . .' I start but she turns back towards me and her face tells me to plug my mouthhole. I do.

'OS says you're due for release, Mahoney,' she says. Her usually flush round face is pale and pinched. 'Now, that could change at any second so, unless you wanna try your luck in a Prisoncorp with the big girls, I suggest you get a wriggle on.'

Aunt Bev turns and hurries up the stairs, lighter on her feet than I'd imagined. I still gape for a second but then I limp after her. I get it but I don't, so I follow her anyway. How is this happening? Is Warden Vile here?

Who changed the Sys? I look at Aunt Bev's giant bum fast-swinging side-to-side with each step, but it's got no answers for me, so I follow, mute, on feet that feel like blocks of wood.

The halls are jammed with kids weaving back and forth. Is it breakfast? Lunch? No, dinner. Processing out always happens after a full day of work, 'cause why not get another day of free labour from us? It's like a last little jab in the side before they turf us out on our arses. I'm trying to keep up with Aunt Bev but all the parts of me hurt and there's this kindling anger in my gut.

Everyone's staring at me with slack-jaws and I realise I'm looking totally knocked around. I stare back at them and think about how little it would take for them to all look like I do, just one step outta line. I hang my head because there's so much pain and rage and shame in me that it must be all across my face, and I can't bear the thought of them seeing that. Emotion is weakness. Weakness is like a big flashing, alarm-wailing beacon here. Even though I'm on my way out, I can't just switch that off.

At the dorm door, Bev points inside.

'Pack your shit, Big Star,' she says as I haul myself past her and into the dorm. 'I'll meet you down in the lobby for signout. Don't dawdle.'

I nod. She doesn't need to tell me twice.

Blondie and Ara come into the dorm after I get

changed, just as I'm throwing my bloodstained night-shirt in the bin.

'Mirii!' Ara says, and rushes to me, pulling me to them and holding me lightly, hands catching in my matted hair and lips pressing to my swollen lips so softly that it's almost like they aren't there at all. Blondie wraps his arms around me from behind and I gasp at the feather-press of his arms around my shoulders. I can feel his lips plant kisses on the crown of my head.

'What did they do?' Ara asks.

'Oh, you know, torture and humiliation. The usual.'

'Bastards,' Blondie says, and he's got tears coming from his eyes and he'd be mopping them up with his shirt if he was wearing one, but of course he isn't. They're probably running in droplets through the ridges of his abs and the thought makes me smile. It stings.

'How did you hack the OS?' I ask, tying my boots to the arm of my backpack.

'It wasn't us,' says Blondie. 'We tried, but they beefed up security, put double A and U's on all the posts on nightshift.'

I'm reaching gingerly into the remains of my mat-tress, feeling inside the twisted hidey-hole and I'm way confused, because if it wasn't them, then who? But something else has got my brain and it's not in any state to be running two strings in simult, yeah?

'Have you seen my tab?' I ask, talking right over Blondie.

'Nah, I thought you'd hidden it in the roof panels with your tattoo stuff,' Ara tells me. 'That's why Vile didn't find it.'

'No, it was here. It was right here.'

There's a little sound from over to my left. Like a laugh or a snort.

I fugging knew it.

'So, Mirii. I'm just reading about that baby magpie chick you found down at the corp in Umina when you were twelve . . . It was really funny how you spent so long raising it and hiding it and feeding it, and then that Uncle found it and cr-'

'Freya,' I hiss.

She's sitting propped up against the wall, legs crossed and my tablet in her lap. She's in her night-shirt already, white cotton in amongst her white sheets, pale skin poking out, pale hair spread over the pillow.

'I logged onto your Free School account,' she tells me, casual as anything. 'Your average was really high, but I did some of your assignments and, yeah, your grades went down a whole lot . . .'

The rage grabs my guts again. There's this pressure inside my head, like my anger is expanding outwards, through my muscles and flash-boiling my blood. I feel the old wound on my cheek, the pulled stitches, start to pulse and ooze with hot blood.

—

I didn't know a body so ruined could move so fast. I don't think Freya knew it either.

—

My hands are around her neck, her eyes bugging and a yelp of shock strangles through her throat, before she even registers that I'm coming for her.

See, I don't just have her by the throat, I've got every fucking Uncle and Auntie and sick-fuck older kid, all the Overseers and the district managers, up to the second-in-charge of Verity House with the plastic face that I met one time at the George Street corp, who shook my hand with a grip like a fresh-coughed hunk of phlegm.

I'm choking out Uncle Jerry from the house out at Orange with his stable of jabber-babes crying for their next hit and Uncle Rick too, who grinned, red faced in the harsh fluorescent of Consequences the other night, as he drove the club against my feet again and again.

I've got Auntie Helen from the Aberdeen corp, a steel-haired, god-bothering old biatch who danced the holier-than-thou jig with one foot while crushing your face underneath the other, and I'm just squeezing, squeezing the life out of her.

I'm pressing my thumbs into the windpipe of Uncle Martin, who gave me a hot little grin as he stamped on the frail body of my little Magpie chick, and I heard its breaking bones and couldn't do anything but be thankful it died quick.

And I've got Vile. I've got Warden Vile round the neck and he's struggling and trying to bat my hands away but I don't let up, won't let up until the black in his eyes spills out and swallows all of him, 'til the black runs out of the pit in my guts to join it.

He gurgles.

She gurgles.

And it's not Vile, or anyone else. It's just Freya, some hard little blonde chicky from the wild Western 'burbs, rounded up but not broke in yet. I look down into her crimson face, those eyes bulging, capillaries popping and the blood spreading out over the whites. In them I see how all *she* knows to do is hurt and rage and thrash out her pain on everyone around her because she can't take it out on anyone bigger. I split-second think about how all *I* can do to cope is turn everything into a big fugging joke but it's *not* a joke and wonder if it's not the same thing, but done different.

Maybe it's *all* the same thing but done different.

Freya punches on, feels the flesh split under her fingers and it helps her to forget. I get it on, and the flesh parts under my fingers and it helps me to forget. Like we're saying it in different ways, but the words are coming from the same place.

And maybe we're too hurt and too scared or too *something* to know that it's not really that she hates me or that I hate her or that we hate each other.

It's that we hate *this*.

So I stop.

I let her neck go and fall back onto the floor and it's like the room comes back. Everyone's frozen, watching. I realise that Blondie and Ara have been trying to pull me off her and so when I fall back, I land on them in this bony, groaning pile of pastel-uniformed limbs.

Freya scrambles to the end of the bed, crouching there with her hair wild and her eyes wilder. She looks at me with fear and awe, then hatred and finally defiance, the emotions changing in her eyes as the colour in her face changes from purple to red to pink then white again.

I hope she never loses that defiance.

I hope she manages to escape soon, 'cause there's no way she's not already signed up for a Prisoncorp the moment she turns eighteen. I hope that the next time she tries to steal away in the night, there's no Uncles on her tail, no close-by newbz to crash-tackle her as she goes past.

'Fuck you, Mirii,' she croaks.

'I'm sorry, Freya.' I am. I'm really sorry, for everything she's had done to her and everything I've been through and all the bullshiz every little bastard in this place has copped and will ever cop.

'Fuck you, Mirii!' she screams.

I reach for the tab and she sees me do it, and reaches out at the same time. She's closer and she snatches it up.

In one swift motion, she raises it up and smashes it against the wall.

It comes apart into chunks, chunks of all the things I've learned and all the stuff I'd cared about and the few contact details I'd managed to keep from kids over the years and some fuzzy pics I'd taken when we'd hacked the camera that one time. The little stories and poems and the bits I wrote out when it hurt too much to keep them inside. Chunks of plastic and steel and solder that she kicks towards me.

But I don't flinch. I don't fall for it. I don't have the urge to dive on her and rip her creamy throat open wide-red with my teeth. Well, maybe a little. But I don't do it.

I just take my pack, boots swinging from the arm, and I turn away.

She hurls a piece of my busted tab, hitting me in the back of the head. My neck rocks forward with it but I don't turn.

'Fight me, Mirii!' she wails.

I want to. I really do. But I don't, too. And all the bullshiz things I could say to her rise up in my throat and they wanna run right out of my mouth but I don't let them.

I keep it to myself because it won't help anything.

—

There are still strings of Freya's hair between my fingers. My hands shake as I brush them against each other, pulling them out. The golden strands float down. They're so fine that I lose them before they hit the floor.

Ara and Blondie fall in line with me as I limp out through the dorm, my feet aching inside my stiff boots and the press of the cotton socks against them almost too painful. Ara takes my bag and guides my arm while Blondie clears a path through the mute throngs of kids gathered around our corner of the dorm.

'Nothing to see here, ya little jerks,' he says, like an Uncle, his voice booming, and the younger ones scatter, giggling nervously while the older ones pull together into groups and whisper as we go past. I can hear Freya swearing and screaming, but the sound of it fades and I try to walk as fast as I can, get far away from her.

Poor Freya. She's like a swirling drain, trying to drag us in and down with her as she empties out. As we go through the door an Uncle comes in, stopping just a second to look at my face with shock and awe, then he pushes past us.

'Ferguson, if you don't shut your hole I'm gunna shut it for you . . .'

The sound of them fades out as we leave the dorm.

It's like I've been holding my breath and maybe now I can release it. It's like I've been holding my breath my whole life and now, maybe now, if I make it outside, I'll be able to take another breath for the first time.

'Mirii!' Cam is just a bobbing head in the after-dinner crowd, but I can't mistake his voice. He comes up close and throws his arms around me. The force of his skinny little body is almost too much to bear, but I bear it anyway and I smile into his hair.

'Your face, Mirii. What did they do?'

I pull back and look at him with mock-shock.

'Shiz! Is something wrong with it?'

He grins and all the freckles on his nose crease.

'Look, I signed up for the Free School. They assigned me a tablet. I've never had one before.' He holds up an old tab, a single crack creasing the corner. It catches the fluorescent light and it blinds me for a second with pure white. 'I've got to scrub dunnies in the pre-teen dorm for the next year for it, but check out how rad it is.'

I do. It's pretty rad.

'Isis seven. Good model. If the screen gets fuggity, recalibrate it to minus three, that helps.'

His eyes glow and I bet he spent all last night

checking out Orion or the best ink recipe for a good, solid line in a fresh tattoo. Good on him.

'I've already had one of the hackies from my dorm show me how to use it. Sticksy. He's really good, like scary good.' Cam drops his voice. 'We wrote that patch that changed your record. They were gonna send you up to a Prisoncorp this afternoon, out to Eramus City.'

My eyes bug out so far that they almost pop right outta my head.

'What? Eramus City? Are you kidding? How did you do it?' I hiss. My heart thumps as I think of how different this day might have been.

'Well, it was Sticksy mostly. I just supervised. He's a fuggin' demon on the tab. I'm thinking of taking over his extra duties so he can teach me.'

'Do it. But be careful. And when you learn how to hack around the firewall, look me up. My email is my name; one "r", two "i"s.'

Cam's lower lip trembles a bit so I take him real soft in my arms and let him spill his eyes and his guts out in tears that soak into my chest.

'Happy Birthday, Mirii,' he says, long string of snot clinging to my shirt and his nose in a gross little bridge.

That's right. I'm eighteen today.

'Thanks kiddo.'

'Contact warning, you two!' grunts an Auntie as

she goes by and we spring apart. Cam wipes his face with a sleeve, tears and snot staining the fabric. Then he takes off down the hallway, skinny limbs pumping. He doesn't look back.

I walk down to admin and I toe the line between in-bounds and out-of-bounds, remembering the last time I was here and my body shudders. Aunt Bev beckons to me, gaze steely.

I turn back, just one last time. I've just remembered.

'Hey, who sent me the note?'

Ara and Blondie look at me like I'm talking nonsense.

'What note?' Ara says.

'When I was in Time Out. You sent the food, and under the mandarin was a note.'

'We sent some meat,' says Blondie. 'But no fruit. We couldn't swing both, not on this limited income,' he says, looking sheepish. 'And no note.'

'Shit.' I turn to Ara. 'It was about Vu. The note said something about *Psynode.* Do you know what it is? They called it *Brainfuckers, Inc.* Said Vu could be there. Said Vile knows.'

'I've never heard of it. Do ya think . . .'

'Raaya? Vu? Maybe. I'm gonna look into it.'

'Me too,' they say and this veil of ferocity slips over their face. Ara's hands start to twitch and they stroke the still-raised, ink-shedding tattoo below their elbow, without realising they're doing it.

'Talk to Cam. I'll look too and we can share info.'

Ara nods, long hair swaying. They pull me into a gentle hug.

'We're gonna find them,' Ara says, then turns and marches off down the hall, head up high and stride vicious. Kids scatter out of their way as they storm back to the dorms.

I look back towards Aunt Bev, shuffling papers furiously and eyeing me. She mouths something that could be 'bury the fudge cup', but is more likely something else.

'I gotta bail. I think my exit is not exactly above the board, if you know what I mean.'

Blondie touches my face.

'Seeya Mirii,' he says, his tanned face kinda sad and kinda happy in that way faces get when things are good and bad at the same time. I don't think Blondie's real good with ambivalence. I think it's throwing him.

'Seeya Blondie,' I say. 'I won't forget that first night. Your mad tongue skillz really helped me feel more at home.'

I touch his stomach one last time, feel the valleys and ridges of his muscles.

'Good luck, Mirii. I hope you find her. You know, Vu.' He turns and goes back down the hall, pausing to jump up and tap the doorframe as he passes through it, the muscles in his back tensing and releasing.

'Good luck,' I whisper, not just to Blondie, but to

everyone. Cam and Ara and Ade and Berry and all the other teeners just waiting it out. The pre-teens racing around the halls, working off the evening buzz before bedtime lock-in, the littlies in the kiddie dorms telling stories, making myths. The bobble-headed blobs in the nursery, probably missing Vu's happy face, no idea that they're in it for the long haul. I hope they make it, even though they probably won't.

I toe the line between in-bounds and out-of-bounds, then I slam across it. No point delaying the inevitable.

—

Aunt Bev has everything done, what with all that time I kept her waiting, so all I need to do is sign a form. I scrawl my name across the tab, my finger dragging on the screen and making the letters spread out, far out of their bounds.

She doesn't hit submit. I reckon she'll wait until I'm out the door. I wonder if Bev will lose her job. I wonder if they have a Time Out for Aunties and Uncles who fugg up. Do they get thrown into cells? Will they hang her by the arms, beat her ribs and kidneys and feet? I don't know. I start to ask her but realise I don't want to know.

'Thanks, Bev,' I say, as she helps me stand up. And I mean it. I try and put it into the words, try to fill them up with all the things I want to say to her but can't.

'Shut up, Mahoney, and get a move on,' she says, but she goes a bit red around the ears. I get the urge to throw my arms around her, but I can't. The whole admin area is full of Aunties and Uncles, all quiet and glaring at us, chewing on sandwiches slowly, or paging through tabs. They know this isn't right but I don't know if anyone knows what to do. Sure, the OS is set in stone, but Warden Vile's face is pretty stony and his fists are too, and maybe they speak a louder truth than what any OS could say.

'Bev, do ya know what you're doing here?' says this beefy old Uncle, coming to stand right over me, looming and making me feel real small underneath him.

'Just following the OS, Jeff. You know how it is.'

'I get it Bev, but I'm not sure the OS is up-to-date, yeah? I got a feelin' that when Kyle comes in tomorrow, he's gonna have some pretty stringent OS corrections.'

'Might be, Jeff, but I'm doing my job. OS says she's gotta go, she's got to go.' Bev looks at him real pointedly. 'I'll cop the flack if there's some sys error I don't know about.'

Uncle Jeff grabs me by the arm.

'You could get Bev into real trouble for screwing with the OS,' he says, squeezing my bicep so hard that the nerves in my arm go fuzzy.

'I know,' I say. 'I haven't.' I'm not lying and I try to twist my face to show it, but I don't know if it comes through or not.

He looks down at me, his face a rough-hewn, stubbled mess, blackheads sprinkled over his nose. His eyes are bloodshot and the smell of potato punch oozes out of his pores. He's so big, his gut pressing into my elbow. He could squish me under his thumb and he looks like he wants to, so I try not to move or breathe or exist too hard under his gaze.

'It's on me, Jeff,' Bev says. 'Don't sweat it, yeah?'

His hands twitch. The vein in his neck throbs once, twice. Things go quiet, kinda white around the edges. Does he know he's one bellow, one gripped shoulder, one 'no' away from spinning my life off one way or the other? A bead of sweat grows heavy on his forehead, spills down his cheek, disappears under his shirt collar. I can almost *hear* it trickling over his slick skin, hear the fibres of his shirt sucking it up. My heart thuds, slow and uneven, skipping a beat that probably stops every clock in the house, jams the works in every systower, blocks all the dunnies, wakes up every blobby bub in the nursery and sets them to scream.

'I guess it's on you, Bev,' Jeff says, passing a sleeve over his sweaty head, turning, and waddling away. He looks back, once, jowls set, mouth twisted.

I don't let him look back again and catch me there.

—

'You made it,' Bev says, taking a deep breath of the warm summer air as she pulls me by the elbow out the door and down the first two stairs. I don't reply, just thud down the steps and onto the street, take a lungful of free air. Free air smells like burning rubber and biofuel exhaust. I look back at Bev, her red hair escaping from her ponytail, red cheeks glowing under the front porch spotlights.

'Got a job lined up?' she asks.

'Nah.'

'How about a place to go?'

'Haven't found one yet,' I tell her, and she shakes her head.

I feel really small out here, uncontained, but free too. It's a scary feeling. I look up into the sky. The moon's coming up, waxing, and there's this soft light cast over everything. No clouds. I pick out Crux, low on the horizon, Acrux burning bright at its foot. The tattooed image on my chest pulls a little like it's trying to get up there and join up with its twin. The ground feels different under my feet and the sky seems like it might never end, like I might just lift off and fall up into it.

I'm holding an envelope in my right hand. In it is a hundred whole credits, the reward for my lifetime of labour.

'*Thank you, from Verity House!*' it says, in bright red and yellow letters.

The night is falling fast and every spark in the sky gets brighter. I think about the city, and Vu, and Raaya, and whatever Psynode is. I think of credits and jobs, dorms and tabs.

I take out the money, stuff it in my pocket and crumple up the envelope, letting it fall away as I take the first steps.

ACKNOWLEDGEMENTS

There are so many people I want to thank, not just for helping me with this story, but for everything.

Firstly, thank you to Kij Johnson and the Clarion West Class of 2014: Adanze Asante, Alexander Berman, Christopher Nickolas Carlson, Curtis C. Chen, Shannon Fay, Folly Blaine, Rich Larson (and thanks for the added motivation, bru), Michael Matheson, Ian Muneshwar, Chinelo Onwualu, Sandra Martins Pinto, Rhiannon Rasmussen-Silverstein, Anthony Bell, Michael Smith (Dad!), Julie Steinbacher (Julieface!), Yang-Yang Wang, Alison Wilgus as well as co-ordinators Micaiah Huw Evans and Neile Graham for digging the original short story *Welcome To Orphancorp* enough to motivate me to extend it. You are all such wonderful people and fabulous babes and your support in Seattle and after has been such a comfort.

Thank you to my other CW14 instructors: James Patrick Kelly, Ian McDonald, Hiromi Goto, Charlie

Jane Anders and John Crowley for everything they taught me about wrangling words into shape.

Thanks to Tim McDivitt and Arcadia Lyons for being my faithful first readers and making me feel like I could keep going when I felt like chucking it in, and I mean the whole writing thing, not just this book.

Thank you to Zoya Patel, David Henley, and everyone at Seizure for loving *Orphancorp* and supporting me through this entire exciting process.

Thank you to the staff of the following cafes for the sweet lattes and letting me steal power and take up seating space while I wrote this: Ray's Café in Brunswick and 1000 Pound Bend in Melbourne, Victoria; The Glass Onion Society in Long Jetty, New South Wales and Café Solstice in Seattle, Washington.

Thank you to my wonderful friends for being rad and amazing and reading my stuff and keeping me going. Sally Clair Evans, Lindsay Charman, Laura Heaton, Ashlea Ross, Patrick Lenton, Wes Chung, Alex Cullen, Gab Snowdon, Alda Ribiero, and so many more. You have all had such an impact on my life and the person I am.

Thanks to Shady Cosgrove, Alan Wearne and John Hawke, and all my teachers at the University of Wollongong Creative Writing program and special thanks to Angela J Williams for shaking me out of my fog and getting me there in the first place.

Even though she can't read English and wouldn't care anyway, thank you to my cat for being marvellous and there for me my entire adult life.

Special, special thanks to Nicholas Joyce for saving my ass and my life and putting up with my shit for all these years. You're such a special dude, you don't even know.

Finally, thank you to my mother, Kellie Myers for the love and the life and for being a strong and complex woman and showing me how to be a strong and complex woman and thus how to make them with my words.

Available online and from discerning book retailers

VIVA LA NOVELLA 2015 WINNERS

Welcome to Orphancorp by Marlee Jane Ward
978-1-921134-58-6 (print) | 978-1-921134-59-3 (digital)

Formaldehyde by Jane Rawson
978-1-921134-60-9 (print) | 978-1-921134-61-6 (digital)

The End of Seeing by Christy Collins
978-1-921134-62-3 (print) | 978-1-921134-63-0 (digital)

VIVA LA NOVELLA 2014 WINNERS

Sideshow by Nicole Smith
978-1-922057-97-6 (print) | 978-1-921134-24-1 (digital)

The Other Shore by Hoa Pham
978-1-922057-96-9 (print) | 978-1-921134-23-4 (digital)

The Neighbour by Julie Proudfoot
978-1-922057-98-3 (print) | 978-1-921134-25-8 (digital)

Blood and Bone by Daniel Davis Wood
978-1-922057-95-2 (print) | 978-1-921134-22-7 (digital)

VIVA LA NOVELLA 2013 WINNER

Midnight Blue and Endlessly Tall by Jane Jervis-Read
978 1 922057 44 0 (print) | 978 1 922057 43 3 (digital)

Printed in Australia
AUOC01n0730080715
268741AU00002B/2/P

9 781921 134586